First published in Great Britain in 2015 by Comma Press
www.commapress.co.uk

A CIP catalogue record of this book is available from the British Library.

ISBN 1905583540
ISBN-13 978 1905583546

The publisher gratefully acknowledges assistance from Arts Council England.

Supported by
**ARTS COUNCIL
ENGLAND**

Set in Bembo 11/13 by David Eckersall
Printed and bound in England by Berforts Information Press Ltd.

JEBEL MARRA

by
Michelle Green

Olivia, Louis, and my colleagues and friends in Darfur
– this is for you.

Contents

Debrief

DON'T GO INTO SUPERMARKETS. No arcades, no chain stores, no automated tellers. Avoid shops. Anything with plate glass walls, reflective surfaces.

Do not allow strangers into your flat. They will knock at your door in twos, smiling, asking if this is a convenient time and if you know about, if you use, if you would like, if you are interested.

You are not. Even though you *are* interested, though you want these strangers, these blank sheet people, want them on your couch nervously checking their watches as you talk and you talk and you talk. Even though they are the first people you've seen all week who do not make you quake with fear by using your name or worse, a pet name, a personal name that they and only they know because they are part of your history. Even though these people are not part of your history and are more beautiful for it, do not allow them into your flat.

Instead, save up your energy and go somewhere remote. Go where the lines on the map get fewer, where the accent changes, where the trees lean away from the sea and the birds huddle on the shoreline, facing the wind. Drink a little. Drink a little more.

When the man at the bar asks about what you've done, where you've been, forget silence and tact and blurt out something about kidnappings on the border of DRC, about child soldiers and janjaweed. His face will be hungry, will be wanting more, asking what, how, thinking he really wants to know. Forget your role as buffer and say it, say that the kids are broken and rebuilt, made into killers, made to bite another child to… stop. Stop talking when his face changes, reaches for another topic, another set of eyes, the barmaid, the floor. How about that game then, eh? You're crap at this. No sense of appropriate boundaries, no ability to read the subtext.

'What was Darfur like?' your next door neighbour will ask, and this time, remember. Read the subtext. Say, 'Hot.' Then she can laugh and you can be spared the look of revulsion at how messy your insides are, at the ugly stains on your memory. Those stains are yours.

Find soldiers, if you can. The man with the bullet wound in his leg, hollow face at the local park, following his physio regime. Find him and sit beside him on the bench by the slide. Don't say much. When he says he'd have shot you if his CO told him to, that's how it works, following orders, just listen. When he mimes a handgun and can't stop swallowing, hold his eye contact. Say something about lentils and compounds and five months in the desert without leave. Say something about all the ex-squaddies turned aid workers, the soldiers in civvy clothes, boots in forty degree heat, and three weeks with the family twice a year. It's enough.

Those people who want you to cry it all out, to spread it all over their living room floors: avoid them. Avoid the confession junkies. Avoid the enquiring eyes, the unsolicited hugs, anyone who claims to know a good counsellor.

Read news online. Collect articles and maps, translate from Arabic, save in a file, keep in a drawer. This is not going away.

When you hear 'That's so brave, I couldn't do that,' or 'I'd love to do aid work,' make a sound that's not a real word, like 'mmm'. Don't get drawn in.

Think about running away again. Don't. Stay inside, triple lock the door, watch the horizon from the small window. Stay inside. Watch the door. Watch the horizon. Stay inside. Stay.

The Red Mountain

SHE WANTED TO KNOW if I was willing to move. She hadn't spoken at all until then, except to say hello as she shook my hand at the beginning of the interview. The other two led the discussion and it wasn't until I felt the questions drying up, about thirty minutes in, that she spoke. I said yes, of course, I would move if it was necessary. A week later I was called in and offered the job by the talkative two. I didn't meet the silent woman again until I arrived in the camp in West Darfur, two hundred miles from home.

Gloria works in the corner of what used to be the village schoolroom, where the teacher would have sat. She still says very little. I'm in the front hallway, on the administration desk. Another school has been built by one of the NGOs, much larger than this little building, and many of the children attend daily. Even so, every road in Mornei Camp is full of small feet running barefoot in the dust. The original village now shelters 80,000 people, more each week, and as it grows the new roads sprawl out, twisting and looping in defiance of the straight line, now so short, that was once the main road through.

My uncle's second wife was born here when it was a village of people all sharing one well, one schoolroom. Her family grew small crops on the banks of the wadi and kept a few animals. A simple life. She moved to El Fashir at nineteen and never tired of telling my uncle how much she hated the city. It was a huge dirty place as far as she could see, and she

3

persisted in this belief right up to her death. She was a child of the red mountain, so she said, and now that mountain is one of the few features of her original home that has remained unchanged. The mountain sits alone, nameless, at the south edge of the camp, its cousins – Jebel Marra – massed far away in the east.

The red mountain attracts stories among those who live beside it. One is that janjaweed fighters are hiding on the other side, ready to kidnap and punish anyone who ventures over that way. The children dare each other to scramble up, running down again from the halfway point, squealing with fear and excitement. The janjaweed have formed their own village, so the rumours say, and no one who has ventured near it has ever been seen again. Every time another person repeats this I want to shout, 'No, they're sitting in the market with what used to be your horse!' but I never do. Everyone prefers to pretend the militias are hidden away behind the mountain, not right there in the middle of the camp, flaunting themselves, laughing and smoking and lying around like they own this whole place.

This week we are preparing for a field survey. I've managed to borrow two tents that we can set up while we're out. It's OK for me to go as I will be staying in the larger tent with Gloria, while Alex and the two drivers stay in the small tent. It's only the five of us on this survey, two vehicles, and we will be away for three nights. I'm excited. I don't mind working in the camp, but my job is getting a lot more interesting now that I am part of the survey team. I'll be doing translation and record keeping, assisting Gloria and the new boss, Alex. My first task is to take their lists of everything we'll need to bring and make sure it's all packed and ready to go by tomorrow morning. Tomorrow we will head east past Zalingei and then north to the villages near the Jebel Marra range. The Bad Mountains – our lonely mountain's kin.

I get one of the drivers to help while the other checks over the vehicles and tops up the oil. The cook makes food for us to take and packs it into the cold storage boxes we've got at the back of the kitchen. Alex has all kinds of equipment piled outside the door to his hut – solar chargers, lamps, measuring devices and more; as he adds to the pile he whistles and sings quietly in words I can't make out. Gloria's in the office tapping on the laptop, finishing up before we go out of range for a few days.

Once I've got the vehicles packed and ready for the morning I walk out to the street. I've got time before dinner, so I take the opportunity to visit my friend Aisha, who's working as administrator for another agency. She's finished for the day, so we share some tea and speculate about Alex's age. She's met him twice and thinks he looks too young to be a boss. I think it's impossible to guess anyone's age. All the international staff look either far too young or far too old. Sometimes they go from one to the other in little more than a year, from all the alcohol I suppose.

There are children in this camp who look older than Alex, older in the eyes. He's only been here for a few weeks and has spent all of that time suffering in the heat, actually walking around with a wet cloth on his head, moaning and puffing like he's about give birth. He's from Denmark. Gloria's from Kenya, I think. Or Uganda. I can't remember. I tell Aisha about how Gloria told him to get rid of the cloth and stop groaning all the time. Sometimes she looks a bit embarrassed by him, but I think he's nice enough, friendly and talkative, so maybe he'll be OK.

It's time for me to head back to the compound for dinner and one last check of the lists, so I bid Aisha farewell and head back home. I do think of it as home now. Not real home, not family home, but work home. A stopping place.

All the displaced do their best to make homes in the camp. The poorest and most alone make fences from torn plastic bags and green sticks, the ones they can't use for fire.

Those who've been here longer have grass matting strung around the sides of their spots, and some even have improvised bricks they've made with mud from the bottom of the wadi. All are ramshackle, whatever material they've used. Ending up here, stringing bags between twigs, is nobody's plan for a life.

As I turn onto the road beside our compound, I sidestep three women with wood and grass bundled high on their heads. They walk in unison and one meets my eye. She is my age, my height, dressed in purple and pink. She looks like my aunt, high cheekbones, Zaghawa tribe, and I am about to say something when reason kicks in and I hold my tongue. Of course she's not related to my aunt. She's almost certainly an IDP, not one of the original five hundred villagers. She's probably Masaliit, not Zaghawa. In fact, who could ever hope to find even one of the original five hundred in this messy blow-away village of 80,000? The women pass and with them my daydreaming. I make my way back to the compound for one final check and then dinner.

In the morning we set off early while the sun's still low in the sky. The whole camp is already awake and the air is thick with the smell of cooking fires. Gloria and I go in the lead vehicle with Alex behind us in the second. The area immediately around the camp is busy, full of people, animals and soldiers. One single tree stands on the camp perimeter, its trunk stripped of its lower branches. The rest of the ground is bare, any bushes and grasses long since harvested to feed the thousands of fires that light up each morning at dawn. We leave the camp and I turn to watch through the back window as the mountain's hidden side reveals itself for a moment, and then disappears again with a bend of the road.

The road is not too bad for the first few hours and we're passing Zalingei by noon. Right before we turn off the main road towards the survey sites, we pass another NGO convoy heading in the opposite direction, three vehicles. Next is a truck piled high with bundles, cases and men. The truck pulls to the edge of the road to let us pass, and as we do, all the men clinging to the sides peer in at us. I peer back. One of them looks out of place in dark trousers, his shirt tied clumsily around his head like a westerner on their first visit. He's the only one not in a jellabiya, and when he catches me staring, I look away. Gloria looks straight ahead.

We turn off the main road and continue for another hour or so, meeting no other travellers. A band of Wadi monkeys race ahead of us, easily outrunning our slow pace for a few minutes, and then they tumble off the road. A small track appears and then disappears every few minutes, and so this is what we follow. We're moving a lot slower now, pausing while Gloria checks and rechecks the coordinates on her GPS. I stay quiet. Every few miles we stop and Gloria asks me to photograph something – an old guard post, an abandoned well. She and Alex scribble notes and compare them during our frequent stops. They're following the aerial surveys we got from the UN, rough maps they've devised from their flyovers, overlaid onto satellite maps. Everything we come across is marked onto Gloria's map, along with estimates of the population. When we can, we speak to the locals. I translate, explain to the villagers, and communicate their responses. Progress is slow, and by 6pm we have surveyed three small villages, all relatively near each other. Kurni is the largest, and becomes our home for the night.

After discussion with the sheikh, we are welcomed to stay in Kurni and invited into the sheikh's home for dinner. We bring some of our packed food and eat with him and his family. I translate for a few hours, through dinner and then for some time afterwards. Sheikh Abdullah tells us that the village has grown in the last year, housing people from across the surrounding area as they flee the janjaweed. The most recent group arrived over a week ago and have been sheltering in an old cow pen until proper homes can be built.

'We will not leave Kurni until death comes right here and grips my hand,' he says, and I believe him. This must be the only place he's ever lived, the place his parents lived and died, and the place in which he intends to also take his last breaths no matter what threatens him and his people. I try imagining El Fashir like that, my own home, and my mind keeps slipping off it like the sole of a shoe on sand. Even when the rebels attacked the airport and destroyed the government planes, I felt we had protection in our city, in our numbers. Not like here; wide open and alone.

The next day we set out after sharing coffee and bread with the sheikh's family. The UN flyover map has several other villages located in this area, so we move slowly towards what looks like the nearest, about fifteen miles away.

An hour passes – a deep gully, a flock of wild chickens and the twisty road – and we finally arrive at the next mark on our tentative map. We are greeted by the scorched black arms of a naked tree, bare against the sky.

The track leading into the village is smeared dark, piles of bone-white ash lying here and there like all the rubbish fires have been moved out to the front, onto the main road for everyone to see. My chest aches. I try to swallow, and it's like something's stuck there, so I just hold my breath.

We stop the vehicles and climb out into silence. We stand still for a long time, watching for movement, coiled tight like hunters, like hunted – listening. Nothing. The drivers sit still in their seats. Nobody speaks, but Gloria beckons us to walk with her, to survey the collapsed remains of this tiny village.

We move slowly. I count six compounds, then seven, maybe eight. The grass walls are spread across the ground in charred tatters and it's hard to see what might have been there before the attack. Broken huts gape like wounds, their roofs collapsed, their walls jagged and torn, only a few feet tall in places and in others completely crushed to dust. Of one, only the frame of the door remains, a wide open mouth. A doorway to nothing; a doorway to ash and filth, to the still remains of a dead home, its throat cut by fire.

I follow Gloria and Alex through the village, stop at each hut, take photos where they ask. Not one sign of life. Not one goat, not one chicken, not a single person.

We approach the last hut and outside a scattering of onions lie across the ground, half-burnt and split open in layers, their inner skins pocked with blisters. This is when I feel myself buckle, when I reach for my mouth.

Gloria and Alex spend a long time back at the vehicles. They contact base with the satphone and talk at length about where we should go next. I sit inside the vehicle with the doors shut, sipping water. The drivers are talking together, leaning on the front bumpers and pointing at each of the destroyed huts in turn, shaking their heads.

All I can smell is burning. Burning grass, burning wood, burning dung, burning hair.

Where are the people? Are they in Kurni? In Sheikh Abdullah's cow pen?

There is no smoke rising from any of the piles of ash and blackened ground, but still that smell. The split onions, and no people.

I get out of the vehicle. Gloria and Alex are still talking, writing things down. I go a little way down the road to where I can see that house with the onion pile. I watch from a distance. Watch the wind move the soil and ash in little circles, watch the blue of the sky pour in through broken roofs, press down on crumbled walls.

Behind the devastation lies a line of bushes, quite far from the village. They look like calabash, seem obscenely green against their foreground, heavy with bitter inedible fruit. My tobe slips back and as I pull it up and secure it over my shoulder, she is there, stepping from the bushes, holding a child by the hand. There.

She stands in front of the bushes staring right at me. The child grabs her leg, tries to climb, and she struggles to lift him. She is there. There in front of the green, behind the huts and the onions and the black smear of road, right there.

At last I find my voice, shout first in Zaghawa, then Arabic, then English. Gloria and Alex have stopped their discussion, the drivers too, and are all moving towards me, looking where I'm looking. There. In front of the bushes, holding a boy.

She is Zahra, her son is Ali. They have been hiding for a week, eating roots. This much she tells me on the way back to Kurni.

She drinks water. The boy eats pieces of fruit and bread and then throws them up on the back seat. He cries a little and his mother wipes his mouth. He eats more bread, keeps it down this time, and then falls into a sudden sleep across her lap.

I speak to her in broken Fur. I don't know much of her language, but she barely talks anyway, just stares straight ahead like she can't really hear me.

'Where do you want to go? Where can we take you?' I ask her, and already I know the answer.

Gloria says we will stop in Kurni, check with the sheikh, find out if her family or her neighbours are sheltering there, and if not she'll come with us to back to the camp, where there are medical facilities and safe water and school and... nothing like that patch of stained ground. Nothing like home. She will come with us to the big red mountain.

'Where do you want to go?' I hear myself say again over the rough growl of the engine – the black armed tree and the ash moving in circles – my mouth making words just for words and I know the answer: for her there is nowhere. The people who did this sit in the market, in the open, and I know if I look on the other side of the mountain I will find it bare.

The Nightingales

WE COME TO YOU live from Geneina, the capital of West Darfur, where the weather this morning is currently a sunny 38 degrees with the chance of rain still holding at nil for the one hundred and seventeenth day in a row. Top story today is from our international news division in Zagreb, Croatia, where one Iva Valentić is celebrating her birthday at home in Dubrava while her shitbag of a boyfriend takes photos of sand in the Darfur desert.

Happy birthday sweetheart! I hope you have a beautiful day planned for yourself.

I know this email is a poor substitute, and I wish with all my heart that I could be with you right now. I did try to phone so that I could sing to you but unfortunately, as the mobile network is down, you've missed out on my harmonic rendition. Sorry to start with the bad news.

The good news, though, is that the internet connection at the UN offices is so much faster than anything at home, and as it's via satellite it keeps working even when the government cuts everything else. I can't make phone calls a lot of the time, or send a single text, but I can shop online and – even better! – write to you. I'll be getting a satphone soon, for when I head out into the bush.

I wish we could spend a decadent day together eating cake in bed. Ah well, until then, have a wonderful birthday. I send all my love.

My dear Iva,

How was your night out with Katja and the others? I did a little toast to you here with some warm Pepsi and a piece of lime from the tree in the guesthouse garden.

I'm still in Geneina (because of the excellent nightlife, obviously). A few days ago I met a man called Bilal at the tea stand near my guesthouse. Really friendly guy, has a warm way about him. He kinda reminds me of Gregor. The same eyes, talks with his hands, and he hums when he's thinking, the same little tune over and over. We ended up chatting for ages and it turns out he's a font of local knowledge. He speaks perfect English, has done a little of everything – driving, translation, a bit of work for some of the NGOs – and, as it happens, his most recent contract has just ended and he's looking for work, so it looks like I've found my fixer, for 4000 dinars a day: slightly *less* than what Marković agreed to. Maybe he'll balance it out by adding the difference to my salary? Ah well, as long as the bean counters of Europapress are happy, I suppose they'll leave me to it.

I spent yesterday with Bilal just covering some basics around the local market: loads of soldiers and truck-mounted machine guns, war junk in the wadi. I also took some shots of people just going about their business, and one turned out really well. It's of these two guys standing in the door of a mechanic's shop – one Sudanese and one white guy. The Sudanese guy has a tuft of salt and pepper beard growing from his chin, styled out to a point, and the hair on his head sticks right up. His face is a relief map with really intense eyes, and he's got a loud, gravelly voice like he's Darfur's answer to Tom Waits. He's throwing his arms up as he speaks and the white guy just stands there facing him, completely still. I can't attach it as the connection keeps dropping out, and I'd rather just get this message through for now, but I'll try to send it soon.

Today we went out to one of the camps on the edge of town where I managed to shoot and interview a few IDPs (internally displaced people – apparently you're not a refugee until you cross an internationally recognised border). Ardamata Camp is pretty big, bigger than most of the others here. We drove around it and went in from the far side, where the road was marked by four enormous vultures sitting hunchbacked in a bare tree. I know I should despise them for the gruesome way they earn their living, but I can only admire these birds. They're statuesque in their own way.

I shot some women returning from collecting firewood and interviewed them too. They had to walk out for miles to find the wood, so by the time they returned it was golden hour and their clothes were like lanterns. I caught them as they passed by the vultures' tree. I know, I know, Kevin Carter and a thousand African photographers roll their collective eyes. I do find myself regularly wondering how to capture anything here without just repeating what's been done before, but I have to push that back, just keep at it. Something worthwhile will emerge... I hope.

On the way back to the guesthouse, I got Bilal to pull off the road and into a potters' yard on the edge of town. They were finishing up for the day, and I wanted to photograph them in the last of the evening light. Some normality in the war zone. They run this little business together, all women, making storage and water filtration pots. Apparently business has been good since the NGOs arrived. I asked them what their husbands do, and they all looked at this one woman, dressed in green.

She told me (with translation from one of the others, a broad woman, looked like the oldest) that she hasn't seen her husband for months, but that he's somewhere near Zalingei, in the foothills of Jebel Marra. 'He's gone to fight for Darfur,' the big woman said, and I remembered Bilal mentioning a rebel camp out there, somewhere in the hills. I told her that we're planning to head to Zalingei, and her friend then launched into this long story about the two rivers crossing in the middle and how it's the most beautiful town in Darfur, apart from Geneina. Bilal chipped in, and soon they were all talking in Arabic, with me and the woman in green just standing there watching them. The big one decided we should have tea with them, so she sent the youngest to boil some water, and then bustled Bilal over to where they'd arranged their best pots for display. It looked like he was getting the sales pitch. I guess they're always working.

While the others were pressing Bilal to buy a pot, the woman in green leaned over and whispered something to me. I only realised it was English the second time. She gestured at Bilal and asked if he was taking me to meet the rebels near Zalingei. More of a statement, really. He was crouched down, running his hands over one of the pots and talking loudly with the big woman. I nodded, told her that's what I was hoping for.

'Take this to them, ask for Asif Yaqub Yawar,' she said, and then she pressed something into my hand. A necklace – black and white and orange beads, with a small metal pendant embossed with script, a quote from the Koran, probably. I stared at it for a moment, until she closed my hand around it. 'Please. Do this,' she said. 'Asif Yaqub Yawar – say it back to me.' I thought about explaining how unlikely it was that we'd cross paths with him, that I didn't even have an interview secured, but instead I just repeated his name and slid the necklace into my pocket as Bilal walked back over, holding a new pot. Why not try to deliver some small comfort to her distant husband? At least it seemed to make her smile.

It's similar to the necklace I sent you a few weeks ago actually, although yours doesn't have the pendant. I think it must be the local style. Has it arrived yet? I hope you like it.

Dear Iva,

The weather report remains as it was, and I still miss you immensely. No change there.

Apparently we need to get a few travel permits before we can leave Geneina, so I've spent the last two days following

Bilal around what seems like every administrative office in town. One good thing is that we've had time to talk, so I made the most of it. I decided to tape an interview with him, just something rough, so that I've got a base for comparison once I start meeting more people.

I asked him to tell me what the war is actually about – basic, I know, but necessary – and he just laughed and said, 'OK, why don't you tell me what you know already.' I told him about what you and I found in our research together: Darfur fighting oppression by Khartoum, all the stuff about the Arab elite targeting the non-Arab tribes in the west by arming the janjaweed militias with money, guns and backup planes, all that. Devils on horseback, the government proxies.

Apparently we've got it wrong. First of all, he says that the devils on horseback thing is a loaded translation. 'It's not wrong,' he tells me, 'but neither is it literal.' The literal translation is something like 'man with a horse and a gun', which could describe about half the town as far as I can see. He then points to an old guy walking at the side of the road and says, 'There: old janjaweed.' Just right there, in front of us, and when I ask how he knows, he says, 'I know him well.' He's always lived here, apparently. Distant relative of the baker down the road from my guesthouse, used to be a herder but has settled in Geneina. He's not a fighter though, this old guy. He's just related to them, so apparently that means he *is* them... I think?

Next thing he tells me is that a lot of the JJ fighters are recent immigrants from Chad. Their tribal affiliations cross the border, so on the promise of money, guns and sex, they come over to do the government's dirty work. Are you getting all this? So far, the janjaweed are killers, except not all of them are, because some are just distant relatives: they're local, and also not local; they are devils, as well as men; and finally, some of them will have known the people they're attacking for years. Generations even.

There's no question that these government-backed death squads are terrorising the locals. They sweep into villages to kill, rape and burn. The stink of murder and much worse hangs over the camp, and even outside - in the eyes of those potter women. But it's so much more complicated than anything you and I read. All of these people are Muslim: the victims, the janjaweed, the rebel fighters – all of them - and the JJ sometimes attack other Arab tribes too. The conflict gets reduced, described simply as 'Arab on non-Arab violence', but that's not quite true. This is regional. It's about power, and land, not some simplified tribal war.

The best I can work out is that what are referred to as 'janjaweed militias' are mostly young men with vague tribal connections to the Arab elites in Khartoum. They've been convinced by the high-ups that the others are thieves, stealing their grazing land, hogging scant resources. They've been told that they and they alone have the ancestral right to the land, and as the desert grows south each year, squeezing everyone, that kind of logic is probably not a hard sell. Does any of this sound familiar, Iva?

According to Bilal, when the JJ aren't killing the non-Arab tribes – 'what you journalists like to call the 'Black Africans',' he says - they're killing other Arabs, and at this point it all starts to break down even further. Arab, non-Arab, 'Black African'–in Darfur they're all neighbours, intermarrying, living together. They're all African. All Muslim. It's less about tribal affiliations and more to do with the fact that Darfurians of all stripes say they've been ignored by the national government. I'm under pressure to boil it down to Arab vs. non-Arab in my copy, like everyone else, but it's not quite right. I don't know how to neaten this, to explain it succinctly. To be honest, I don't quite understand it.

Hi sweetie,

Sorry about yesterday's incoherent rant. My head's not spinning quite as much this morning, and I've woken up to some good news: the travel permits are all signed and stamped and we are free to go!

Bilal knows that I'm after an exclusive, something big that will draw attention back to this place, so after a bit of what he called 'sniffing the air', he took me to meet Irshaad. Irshaad is as big as our wardrobe and about as talkative. Never takes his sunglasses off. He won't deal directly with me, but according to Bilal he has links with the Sudanese Liberation Front. He's agreed to take us to meet them for interview. They are one of the many groups fighting the JJ and their government masters. They've released a couple of press statements since breaking away from the Sudan Liberation Army – regional autonomy, demands for power sharing and representation in Khartoum, that kind of thing – but they tend to stay well hidden for the most part.

This particular unit is based north of Zalingei (you should be able to see it on the map I left – it's above Jebel Marra, the large green patch east south east of Geneina) and although they are pretty much permanently mobile, to avoid attack from the government and JJ troops, some of their number have agreed to meet us. My ultimate goal is to interview Colonel Masood, head of the SLF for the region. No one from the press has spoken with him directly, so if I can tape an interview, I should be guaranteed coverage for it.

I'm seriously regretting my lack of equipment. I've got decent audio, and my DSLR can take short pieces of video, but it's not really broadcast standard. I suppose it will be fine for field quality. Marković didn't want to pay out on a whole team for me, especially since the main international focus has shifted to Ache and the tsunami, but he did set up a link with one of the UN comms teams for file transfers and basic support, so I guess that's something. I am, essentially, a one man band. I'll work with what I've got. I've already sent the camp profiles back, as well as the Khartoum collection I sent to you, but I need something more. I don't see the IDP profiles as a waste of time per se, but I'm afraid they'll have little impact on his editorial highness. So far I've only interviewed people in the camps around Geneina – displaced families, widows and orphans. Many of them have fled more than once. I ask why they left, how they got here, and then I set up a photo. It all gets sent back to either sit in Marković's inbox or, at best, be filed away with forty other human interest stories that may or may not get used as a sidebar deep in the international section of the website - if I'm lucky. Since the damn tsunami, the agenda has shifted and Darfur is out. This is why I need an interview with the rebels. I need something big. I need to be where the action is.

Oh, and before I forget again: my satphone finally arrived! It costs a huge amount of money to call in or out, so unfortunately I can only use it for work and emergencies. The number's at the bottom of this message, in case you need it. Please though, don't call unless it really is urgent, as it'll cost you a fortune. While I'm away from Geneina and the luxury of internet access, I will keep writing to you in my diary, and when I get the chance I'll tear the pages out and send them through Irshaad's brother-in-law – he owns a bookshop in the centre of Geneina. Of course, once I'm back in town I'll be able to email you again too!

Please give Mica a cuddle and a long scratch behind the ear from me.

Take care, gorgeous – I love you.

I've left my laptop and all but one of my notebooks in the guesthouse safe, so in the interest of keeping a record (and travelling light) I'm just going to write it all here for the both of us. Sorry, this isn't much of a letter.

Okay. Here's what I have so far: Irshaad, Bilal and I arrive in Zalingei late afternoon and go to a house on the outskirts of the town where we are welcomed by a family known to Irshaad. Karim is the patriarch of the household, an old Zaghawa man who has lived his whole life in this valley.

He's a millet farmer now, with a small herd of camels left over from his father's days as a trader. His son Abdulatif comes to meet us, and after we eat, we sit with the two of them. Abdulatif is an old friend of Irshaad's, and he is with the SLF. He joined them after it became clear that he had the wrong tribal connections for a successful career in the Sudanese Army. He wears a string of amulets around his neck, folded pages from the holy book bound tight inside leather packages. Spiritual armour, I suppose.

I ask him about the columns of young men I saw marching out from Geneina in the still hours of the early morning.

'Ah yes,' he says, 'we trained at night as well, when it was cooler, and then we'd sing songs challenging the sun to rise and face us.' He laughs, looks embarrassed. 'Arrogant, like young men are.' He is forthcoming and open to talking about his experience in the Army, particularly his time in South Sudan, but when I ask what one does as a young cadet, the detailed answers stop and he just says, 'You go to war.' Our conversation eventually settles and we are ushered to our beds.

I don't sleep much. I spend most of the night working over my questions for Colonel Masood, in the hope that I eventually get to meet him.

In the morning, we are fed and watered, and sent on our way. We leave with Abdulatif and drive east from the town, and as we approach a checkpoint on the road I find myself fingering the string of beads in my pocket.

The sun is high overhead when we finally pull over into a lay-by of sorts, a wide patch where the road becomes a tangle of smaller tracks that wind out into the hills. Irshaad radios ahead, a short, vague message, and twenty minutes later we are met by three soldiers in a converted truck. After a brief greeting, we drive in convoy down one of the smaller tracks, a tenuous road that leads to a sheltered hillside. This isn't their main camp, at least not for now, but I am told we are no more than ten miles away. This is another checkpoint, some kind of outpost for the rebels. The three who meet us are stationed here while the rest of their unit keeps moving.

The soldiers pull their vehicle around and park it facing out, the enormous barrel of the mounted machine gun stretching through what had once been a cab and windshield, pointing back to where we drove in.

'So, Bosnia,' one of the three soldiers says.

'Yes, well, Croatia too.'

'How do you like Darfur?'

The other two don't speak English, so I talk primarily to Sami, the head of this tiny outpost. He and Abdulatif have known each other since childhood. Both joined the Army, both deserted. They interact with the warm familiarity of brothers and tell stories in tandem, seemingly for each other as much as for anyone else. The conversation turns to family and lineage, and they want to know about mine. I tell what I can, the pieces I know, and of you too. The future we hope for. I show them the picture of you on the hill near the observatory, that one where you're all in red.

Abdulatif goes with the other two soldiers to check the maps spread over the bonnet of the truck, leaving the rest of us alone. I remember the necklace. I pull it out and tell Sami what the potter woman said. 'She wants her husband to have it, a good luck charm, a token of love, I suppose.'

Sami recognises the name I've written in the cover of my notebook, says we can take it to him, that he's stationed at one of the checkpoints in the countryside. He studies the pendant and smiles.

'Ah, yes. "*Your heart shall feel no fear, know no sorrow.*" Here are his initials, on the back. We'll take this to him, no problem,' he says, and Bilal leans in to look as Sami hands it back to me. 'You hold it, for now. If we can't drive you there, I'll deliver it myself.'

They don't light fires after sunset, so we retire to our nets quite early. I lie there in the dark for a while, wondering if the man on the necklace misses his wife as much as I miss you right now. The bats fly low, catching the night bugs that gather above my net, and I fall asleep to the sound of their bodies slicing through the air.

We leave just after sunrise the next morning and drive for about 30 minutes before turning off onto a side road, where Sami pulls his truck over and waves us in. A small brick hut stands on the left, built exactly like the ones in their outpost.

'You want to see who we're fighting?' he says, and he ambles over to the hut.

I jump out, and Bilal stays in our vehicle, just leans out the window and watches us.

To the side lies the body of a man in uniform, almost identical to the rebels. He is arranged against the wall as if he is sleeping, propped up in a drunken slump, his head on one shoulder and his palms up. I don't lift my camera, but shoot where it hangs. I walk around the body while Sami talks.

'Janjaweed,' he says. 'He was found by one of our guards in the night. A scout. Periodically they come to assess what we've got, how many of us are in a particular area.'

His clothes are stiff, washed dark, the collar jutting awkwardly away from his neck. His head scarf trails a pale path along the ground beside him.

I ask if he recognises him, if he's known, and he says no, that most of them are from over the border in Chad. 'That's one big problem that the government faces: most of Sudan's ground troops are from Darfur. Not recent immigrants, but rooted here, you know? Good for fighting in South Sudan, not so good for here, so they send in these dogs. Give them weapons and money, tell them they can take whatever and whoever they like.' I crouch down and pull a badge on his shirt into focus. It's obscured by blood, and one corner hangs, a little frayed. The lens flare melts his shoulder.

'We would have held him for questioning but he fought, so his throat was cut.' Sami spits, and then pauses for a moment while I finish up. 'One more camel for our camp,' he says, and he walks back to the truck, the dead man staring after him.

This afternoon I am meeting Masood, commanding officer for the SLF battalion for the Zalingei and Jebel Marra localities. He has agreed to speak with me after receiving my credentials from Bilal and Irshaad. I am told that I have 30 minutes. It's noon when we arrive at the remote clearing that will serve as our meeting room, high up in the hills. Carpets are arranged beneath the few trees, and several uniformed men step forward as we approach. Armed guards stand at each of the cardinal points, and we are waved over to the shade.

Masood talks on a satphone while I set up the audio recorder and check the battery on my camera.

'Colonel Masood, I'm honoured to be able to take your first interview,' I say when he finally hands the phone back to one of his men. He smiles. 'If it's OK with you, we'll record audio, take some still photos, and some short sections of video too.'

'Of course. We want help to spread our message and bring attention to our struggle.'

I hit record.

'I am here in the foothills north of Jebel Marra, one of the rebel-held areas of Darfur – a liberated area, as it is known – and am talking with Colonel Masood of the Sudanese Liberation Front. So, Colonel – can you please tell me about the primary goals of your movement?'

He straightens his shoulders and looks across the lens. His face is relaxed, and he talks with a slow confidence. He's older than I expected, maybe as old as the groups of men I saw populating the tea stands in the Geneina market, but while they seemed hampered by stiff joints and tired hearts, Masood has a lightness about him. His eyes are quick, and each gesture precise. He tells me about the need for political equality and investment, about the economic depression that has smothered his people for generations now, and as he talks, he counts his points out on his fingers. 'The Khartoum government treats us like errant children, and then feigns outrage when we resist.' His men nod as he raises his hand and snatches at the air. 'The British and the Egyptians left in '56, but still in Darfur, we are a colonised people, ruled from the Nile.' The wind catches the mic and roars through the headphones. I cup my hand to its side and lean in a little.

'What are your demands?' His men lean forward when I ask this, but Masood remains still. I push the shot in so that he alone is framed.

'Our first demand is a halt to the attacks on our villages. The janjaweed must be disarmed, and the aerial bombardment stopped. Once this has taken place, we need a peace deal that recognises the political legitimacy of our movement, and that of each of the groups representing the Darfurian people. Not like the N'Djamena agreement that shut out millions and achieved nothing. We need something solid, something that shows significant concession to our needs. Only then, once an agreement has been signed and a ceasefire honoured, will our people return home.'

We've barely begun when one of his advisors brings the satphone back to him – another call. I pause the recorder and begin to get up to give him privacy but he waves me still.

'Forgive me,' he says as he finishes the brief call, and then before I can lead again, he has a question of his own. 'Now let me ask you something: when did you leave school?'

'I was eighteen. I finished my exams and then studied journalism at university.'

'Good, good. I attended the oldest school of medicine in Sudan, at the University of Khartoum. I had the opportunity to complete my education in the capital, and as I'm sure you know, I then practiced at the University Hospital for many years.' He leans back a little and looks to the treetops as he recalls his time there, wanting to know if I've heard of his colleagues and other prominent Darfurian scholars in the capital. I panic a little at the holes in my knowledge, but there's no need, as he goes on, eventually talking me through a short history of the development of the psychiatric profession in Sudan. I'm worried about the time, about getting what I need for this interview, and as I am about to interject, he swiftly returns to the present.

'Are you aware that most of our school teachers are unpaid?' I nod, and he continues. 'Most of them are volunteers. In fact – Ahmed! Please.' He waves over one of his men. Ahmed stands tall at the Commander's side, his hands clasped. 'Ahmed is the Communications Officer for this unit. He was a teacher in his village, Kurni, not far from here. His pupils were those whose families could afford to keep their sons in school. He survived on donations from his students' families – no salary, just spare food, handouts. Can you see how ridiculous that is? When they could no longer afford to have their sons learning instead of working, the students disappeared. The girls left school years before. So, the question I ask is: what is a teacher with no school?' A small gust blows up a corner of the carpet; only the wind answers. 'He joined us four months after it closed.'

He lets the story hang there for a moment, holding the pause with precision. He leans towards the camera now, just a bit, although he still looks across the lens at me. 'What we need is to make a connection between our suffering here and the people in the rich world. We need them to listen, and to act.'

At this, his advisor appears again at his side: another urgent call on the satphone. As he takes the call I move back a little and take a few stills. His advisor nods at me and waves his hand as Masood stands and walks away from the gathering beneath the trees. A small herd of camels sit in the sun at one side of the camp, stoic like the vultures. Several of Masood's men wait by the vehicles, and every minute or so, the guards signal to one another, one by one, clockwise around the camp perimeter. I wait for one of them to raise his hand again and I frame it, finger pointing up, barrel down. I walk out to the far side of the small camp, to where the hill crests and the surrounding countryside lies open and visible for miles around. I shoot the landscape and then spin back to the camp. Masood is standing out in the sun, still talking on the phone, while his men move the carpets so that they're better covered by the shade of the trees. This command centre can be rolled up and stowed in no more than a few minutes. Completely mobile.

That night, I sit beside the pitched mosquito net that serves as my tent and I transcribe our conversation. The potter's necklace rests in the palm of my hand, and I count off the cool beads as I write. I save the new material to the memory card and then remove it, slide it down into the gap in the spine of my notebook. I zip the necklace inside the secret pocket on my cargos and wonder if I'll meet the man for whom it's intended.

I wake in the chill of the early morning to the sound of snuffling near the head of my net. Small feet scuff the ground beside me, something crunches. The sound of chewing. I freeze for a moment, open my eyes wide, and see nothing in the dark. Whatever it is, it's in no hurry, and once it finishes eating, it ambles away before I can reach for my torch. In the morning, little footprints map out a busy night around me. The trail leads off into the bush.

'Colonel Masood has unfortunately had to leave, but you are welcome to travel with us to Zalingei.' Sami stands over me, a cup in his hand. 'He sends his apologies but thanks you for meeting with him. He's a very busy man. I'm sure you understand.'

'Of course, of course.' I wipe the sleep from my eyes, squint up at Sami.

'If you need any further information, I will be happy to help.' He glances down at the sand beside my net and smiles. 'Looks like you've made friends,' he says, drawing the toe of his boot along the sand where the footprints are, and before I can ask him what it was, he walks back to the fire.

I sift through my notes from the previous day; it's not as in depth as I might have liked, but with additional detail from his men, I should be able to pull it together.

The camp has already been dismantled, and only Sami's truck and our battered old Land Cruiser remain. We eat a modest breakfast and are packed in no time.

The drive back to Zalingei takes a different route than the one we came in on. These desert tracks are numerous and subtle, and I count the offshoots as we pass. Irshaad rides ahead in the rebels' truck, gesturing with his hands as he talks with Abdulatif.

Beside me, Bilal chats about music. He pulls a cassette from his pocket and passes it forward to Sami. 'Here. Put this on.' He smiles conspiratorially into the rear view mirror as Sami slides the tape in and hits play. We are blasted with a tinny beat, female vocals singing in close harmony over the top.

'Al Balabil!' Sami shouts. 'My favourite!' He claps the steering wheel. 'I was raised on this. In fact, I'm sure these songs taught me to speak.'

Bilal turns to me. 'So, do you know them? Their name means "The Nightingales".'

'The Supremes of Sudan! Huge!' Sami shouts from front.

The two of them sing along without waiting for my answer, and one verse later I'm bouncing my head to the beat.

The next song begins and Sami lets out a sigh of affection. 'Ahh, 'We Walked, We Walked'.' He lifts his hand as The Nightingales voices rise. 'Now this is relevant to the subject of your article,' he says. 'Many of their songs are about migration. They have a deep rapport with the road, these women.' He watches the landscape for a moment and then continues. 'We Zaghawa are nomadic, partly, like the Arabs. Lots of herders. The Fur and the Masaliit are the farmers. The irrigation that you see in Geneina, Zalingei - the brick factories, the orchards – most of them are theirs. Migration is not their way, but now,' he sucks air through his teeth, 'of course it is forced on us all.' We sit in silence as Al Balabil sing us around the edge of a hill. We pass a stand of trees and low bushes. The song changes and Bilal hums along. I recognise this one, think I've heard him humming it before.

The land is levelling out as we head west, away from the rebel stronghold. We've been driving for a few hours now and ahead of us Irshaad and his friend have pulled their truck over to the side of the road for a rest break. We pull up behind them. The wind has picked up and is blowing from behind, pushing us to Zalingei. It lifts the sand and pelts the bare skin of my hands, snatches Irshaad's voice away as he shouts to us.

'What?' Bilal shouts back.

'Let's pee and get moving. Five minutes,' he says, and he strides into the trees ahead.

Bilal leans down and fiddles with something on the floor of the truck, singing that last Nightingales song while the rest of us find a spot to pee. I grab my bag and walk a little way from where Sami is standing. The ground rises slightly, and with the trees at my back I've got a nice view of the road we've just come down. I put the bag down for a moment, and walk to the edge of the rise. A few nice shots – generic, but they might be useful somewhere. The wind is getting worse, sand now bouncing off the lens, so I stash my camera back in its case, and as I go to unzip my pants, my scarf whips up and flattens across my face, the end flapping around my neck. I fumble with the material as I search for the edge, and through the sound of my clothes slapping in the wind I hear a shout, probably Irshaad calling us back. I find the end of the scarf and pull it back from my face and as I turn to shout back, two things happen in near synchronicity: there is a breath in, quick and sharp, right beside me, and from the direction of the vehicles a single shot is fired. As I turn to face it, the world stops.

The first thing to return is smell. I still can't see, can't seem to open my eyes or focus on any of the muffled swirling sounds around me, but clear as anything, that smell. Two layers of acidic tang, like a nightclub toilet. Piss and cigarette smoke. I let it bring me back, follow it through a fog of sensation to the next detail: pain. It radiates down across my face, deep into my head. Somewhere below this, a separate flurry of signals emanates from my wrists. I can get my fingers to move a little, but they seem to be bound behind my back. I am lying on my side, my feet bare.

The rest stop, the trees. The details inch back.

Two rough voices speak in an unknown language. Is it Arabic? I don't know. I don't even know the language of my captors, can't focus on it long enough to pick anything out. 'Awwww!' they both say at the same time, and then they laugh. The flutter of cards, a dovetail shuffle. One of them bangs the deck against the table and I flinch at the sound, stifle a gasp when my shin cracks against something hard. The men stop talking.

I'm hauled to my knees, still unable to see, arms behind my back, and the two of them yank me one way and then the other. One of them shouts while the other grunts encouragements to his partner. Now both are shouting, one on each side, shoving me with each statement. A blow lands on my face, an elbow perhaps, and I feel my cheekbone crack. I hit the dirt and stay on my side as they kick, try to keep my face tucked close to my chest for the rest of the beating. They stop after a while, ease off as if they're bored, and then go back to the cards. Bandits or soldiers? JJ? The Army? My nose is full of blood. I try to push out the clot with a short firm blow, but it won't shift. I run my tongue over my teeth and there's still just that one missing on the left side, the old gap, nothing more. The men bang the cards down again and I am pulled back to my knees. More questions. I spread my legs this time, keep my head down, and frantically search for the few Arabic words I know. Anything. The shouting stops. They are quiet for a moment and I breathe into the space, prepare myself for whatever comes next. Surely they will want to talk, to question me, find out that I'm no threat to them – oh God. My camera, the transcripts. The desert blows into my mouth, into the space where my words should be, and as a new layer of panic rises, one of the men steps forward. Something small and hard presses into the base of my skull. I feel it make contact, hear the safety, click click.

My panic slows and time becomes elastic. Thoughts crash into each other, a useless pile that I can't pick through. Something else is growing, something deeper. Visceral instinct, and now I am animal, every hair on my balding pelt rising, muscles tightening. I smell my skin, the sharp tang of my trousers, and behind that, the saccharine scent of a rotting thing. I am motionless, feeling the day bend. The man at the end of the gun speaks, calmly this time, with the even pace of finality, and the sound of his voice loosens something in me. It rushes forward. The call from the loudspeaker at the end of the road, my first home, Sarajevo and the sound of the early mornings of childhood: the words are there, they are on my tongue and they are flowing from me now. I reach the sixth verse, prayer is better than sleep, prayer is better than sleep, and at this, the end of the barrel lifts away from the base of my skull. Khalas. I recognise that word. He tells the gunman to stop, and I begin again. I keep repeating, and as I do, they turn to one another and begin debating. The conversation goes on as I repeat five more rounds of the azan.

'Stop,' one of them says in English, and I do. I am lifted and sat on a chair. Two hands press my shoulders down and the space in my mouth feels vast, my throat open and dry, lips like wood. They walk away talking, and with their voices at a distance I wonder how far I'd get if I ran, blind, arms bound. A few hundred feet? I'd probably hit a wall, get shot. I sing the azan to myself quietly, my lucky charm, but it becomes more like hysterical muttering. I can hear the panic in my voice and it doesn't help. Where are they? Where am I?

Ten minutes, fifteen at most and they're back. When the blindfold is lifted I can see nothing but bright light for a moment. His outline appears first, and the details emerge as my eyes adjust. He wears a dark beret. Another stands behind him. The hands on my shoulders release.

'My men say you speak the words of God. Our call to prayer.' He stares at me, his voice even and quiet. 'Is that what brought you here? The words of God?'

I open and close my mouth a few times and he squats down in front of me, looks up into my face. He smiles.

'I'm a journalist,' I finally manage to say. 'I take no side.' He laughs as he stands straight again and looks around at his men as if I've just told a joke.

'OK, journalist,' he says. 'Where's your team?' I don't answer him, just look down at my lap, try to get my breathing under control. He cups his hand under my chin and pulls my face up to meet his. 'Where's your team?' He holds me there. 'Your cameraman, your sound man?'

'I don't have one, don't have them. It's just me.'

'Just you, with your one camera?'

'Yes.'

He laughs again, and my head shakes in his hand. 'How do you know Bilal?' He stands there holding my head, and I don't speak. I can't. I'm silent, he is silent. Nobody moves. Ten seconds like eternity, and then he moves his hand from my chin to my chest.

'How do you know Bilal?'

He waits for a second and then pushes his thumb against the middle of my chest, slow and firm, and the pain bursts through me; something's sticking me, sticking inside me like a knife. Something's broken. He eases off and then pushes again and it forces my voice. I can't stop it.

'He's my guide,' I gasp. 'That's all.' Is this betrayal? This tiny piece of information? It doesn't mean anything, it's... it's neutral. The man in the dark beret leans in till I can see the pores on his nose.

'That's all?' He holds himself one inch from my face, his teeth glinting at the bottom of my eye line. My chest is on fire. A wave of nausea floods through me.

'Yes, yes.' He holds my chin again and leans into my chest once more, slower this time, and I just keep talking. My mouth runs. 'We met in the market, I hired him. He's just a guide. He – '

'Just a guide? Just a guide who managed to bring you to the rebels, just a simple man in the market?'

His thumb goes in, and in, and this time the spike of pain goes all the way down each limb too, through my whole body till it feels like it's pushing out, radiating all around me, and he won't stop asking that same question, again, again, in his quiet voice, his office voice, and all of me is burning raw, screaming. The world spins.

I don't know when it stops, exactly. My head falls when he lets go of my chin and the man in the beret walks away. I brace myself for the next stage, forbid myself from imagining. He walks away without looking back. His men lift me from the chair and I feel my hope drain into the sand at my feet. This is it. The blindfold is tied again, a bottle held up to my mouth, the water splashing down my chest, and they are pushing me forward. What do I do? What preparation can there be? I am lifted into what must be the back of a truck, pushed to the floor. I curl my feet away from the burn of the metal as the tailgate is slammed shut and all I see from inside the blindfold is your face. Your mouth is moving and there's a piece of pepper stuck to your tooth but I don't say anything because I don't want to break the spell. The early days. You are telling me about the elliptical orbit and how it plays tricks

31

with our logic about summer and winter, and the tattoo on the inside of your arm says 23.4 degrees and I realise, this time. I didn't before, when it happened for real. I thought it was the temperature, something to do with the climate, the seasons, I don't know, it seems stupid now that I remember, but this time I know, it's the tilt, the tilt of the earth, so I open my mouth, right now, I open my mouth to tell you and instead of words the wind is there again, punching in and extinguishing my voice without effort like it's the flame of a guttering candle. The moment becomes one of those voiceless dreams that flattens me. I shout and I shout and nothing at all comes out. My head hits the side of the truck as the engine gears up and I am driven out into what I am sure will be the last terror I will know.

I waited until the sound of the engine had retreated before I lifted the blindfold. Hours in the back of the truck, hours, it must have been, because eventually the sun sank and night was on us and still they drove and drove. They pulled me out at some point – I remember my toe catching on the tailgate – and they put me on the ground, pushed me back against something hard. Talked over me for a long time, and then cut my bonds and drove off. I strained to hear the last of their engine and then, after waiting some more, I lifted the blindfold. Only then.

I was under a tree. Beside me, my shoes, with a bottle of water standing in one of them. I didn't drink it right away. Maybe it was poisoned. Just a few drops on my lips at first, careful, and then fuck it, gulped it down, half of it hitting my shirt. I sat there for a long while, touching each bit of my body, something crunching and shifting under the skin of my chest, burning pain with each breath. My left arm wouldn't move. The sun came up and there in the distance were the white things, shimmering. When the medics found me I remember looking down and seeing my shoes on my feet. I was standing. Must have walked. They were Dutch, these two doctors, nurses, I remember that, remember them telling me, and the next time I woke they were both standing over me.

I have been in the medical compound for three days now, those shimmering white tents. They tell me I'm in Chad, just over the border.

Since the kidnapping I have slept very little. I feel awake like never before, and it does not feel good. There is a sickening immediacy to my every thought, as if that gun still rests on the base of my skull and I'm once again searching for words. I expected an interrogation about the interview with Masood, my diary, but all they wanted was Bilal. They just wanted Bilal. I can only guess that they let me go because of my skin. Dead white guys attract unwanted attention from the outside world, but the others have no such protection.

They were expecting us. They knew we'd be on the road at that time, even that we'd stop at that one place. There's no way it was a random encounter, just bandits on the road. No way. They knew who we were and where we were. They knew about the rebels, and that Bilal was with them.

Somebody gave him up, to the army, to the janjaweed, whoever the kidnappers were. Somebody knew.

I try to think this through and see what I've missed. I'm remembering it now: when we stopped on the road, Irshaad disappeared into the trees before everyone else, got out of the way like he would have if he knew what was coming. It was his connection that hooked us up with these guys in the first place. He could have alerted someone to it – the JJ, whoever he's working for. Creepy fucker, that's what I thought right from the start, but I guess I didn't want to acknowledge it, too eager to follow the lead. He barely said two words to me this whole time. Who knows where the hell he is now.

The others. I can't really rule them out either. There's Abdulatif: best mates with Irshaad, best mates with Sami, and formerly of the Sudanese Armed Forces. Great cover for a spy – buddy buddy with everyone, pretend to defect from the

SAF, make a show of your devotion, and then hang it round your neck for everyone to see. He was the only one wearing amulets, now that I think about it. Is that normal? I don't even know.

Then there's Sami. He seemed legit, if not a little desensitised, but then who isn't in a war? That JJ scout he killed though, parading around a dead body. Sami said he was JJ, but he was wearing practically the same uniform as the SLF. Could have been a fucking farmer for all I knew. In fact, now that I think back, there wasn't as much blood as I would have expected. Shouldn't there have been loads more blood if his throat were cut? What if he died of dysentery, or a heart attack or something, and Sami set it all up just to look convincing?

One thing seems certain: one of the rebels is not a rebel.

The doctors are keeping me here. They say they're worried about infection. I woke up fuzzy-headed from the medication this morning, and they handed me my bag, the one I dropped in the bushes. Apparently a man gave it to the night watchman at the compound gate, didn't say his name. Could it have been Bilal? Inside was my diary, with the backup memory card pushed down into the spine. No camera of course, the kidnappers got that, but one of my friends must still be alive. One at least. The doctors let me use their computer, and when I checked the card, it was all still on there - the video and audio files, my rough copy. I've sent it all through to Marković. The doctors said they'd help with my passport, with getting me home. Afterwards I tried contacting the guesthouse in Geneina to see if they'd heard from Bilal, but the network went down. Must be a military strike. Always is when the world goes silent.

A week has now passed and I'm anxious to get back to Geneina. I feel so strange - like I'm falling, like slow dream falling, gravity pulling me back through the atmosphere. My skin burns. The glands in my neck have swollen up and swallowing is a matter of concentration. Numbness is eating me. It creeps up through my neck, across my chest, and it wasn't until this morning that I felt what lay at its base. Fear. Fear with its own identity, almost a separate being that is crawling in through the numbness, wearing me like a suit. I woke up shaking last night and I haven't been able to stop.

Dear Iva,

I don't want you to worry. I write this to calm your concern, though I don't know when or how it will get back to you.

Since my last entry, there is one thing I now know for sure – it can't have been Sami who sold us out. I am told that his body was found not far from where I was dropped, his throat cut, like the JJ scout. No one saw anything. They've known for a few days, the doctors, but only just told me now. Said they didn't want to upset me.

I'm afraid that the next body found will be Bilal's. I try to imagine he's still alive but I can't see how. As long as I'm stuck here, I can't find him, can't help him.

I checked my emails today and according to the latest security briefing, there was a janjaweed attack on Ardamata Camp a few days ago, and two more a few hours later: one was a massive strike against an SLF unit in the foothills of Jebel Marra, a firefight, and one was an air and ground attack on Kurni, that village in the rebels' region. Many people are dead, or missing. There is no confirmation that the attacks were deliberately coordinated but the UN and AU are working on the assumption that they were.

I can't figure out exactly how these are connected to our kidnapping, but they must be. It's there somewhere: the place we came from, the place we went to, both rebel areas. I tried talking to one of the doctors about this, to get him to send me back over the border with the next convoy, but he is resistant, keeps telling me I need to rest, that I am too ill.

The second issue is Marković. I sent the interview materials off to him as soon as I could, once they had been recovered. The connectivity has been patchy but I have still have no confirmation that the story has gone out. He isn't returning my messages and I can't find anything on any of the syndicates. Masood was clear: he needs the support of the international community in order to turn this situation around. I tried emphasising this in the twelve emails I sent to my so-called fucking editor, but all I get back is a message from HR telling me that they're booking me on a flight as soon as possible. They just want to pull me out. I'll try phoning him again tonight. Perhaps if we can speak I can move it forward. I'm trying to stay calm, but it's difficult not to feel furious when I look and look at each of the sites and see nothing significant about Darfur. Last time I checked, the top story was pictures of Brad Pitt and Angelina Jolie on holiday in Kenya.

Iva,

I finally managed to get onto one of the convoys. I have been in Geneina for a week now and can find no trace of Bilal, Irshaad, or Abdulatif. I went to Ardamata Camp yesterday. The residents and aid workers are piecing it back together following the attack. The school was burnt to the ground, seventeen people killed. Many more are missing, mostly women. I went back to the potters' to see if they've heard from any of them, and the one who gave me the necklace just kept saying the same thing again and again: did he get it? Did he get it? When she started crying the older one shouted me away, told me not to come back.

I received a message from Marković today. The story isn't useable. None of the footage is good enough, or appropriate, or some shit. He says I can work it up as part of a retrospective piece for the website when I get back, a blurb for the Sudan page.

I'm not going to think about that right now. There is no room for indulgence, or pointless speculation, so I am simply rewiring myself. To call it self-preservation is not quite correct. That sounds too still. It's more of a re-routing. I may be over-thinking this, but I want to commit it to words, with you as imagined witness, so that I might refer back to this map when the time is right.

I phoned Abdulatif's family yesterday and they told me he is dead. His body was left on the outskirts of Zalingei, tied to a tree. They found him a week before the attack on his unit.

This means my first instinct was right. It was Irshaad. He was the one who gave us up.

My involvement set something off, some chain of events that I don't fully understand. All I know is that the attacks and the kidnapping weren't random. They can't have been.

I spent all of last night debating whether or not I can confront this head on, from here. Maybe if Bilal was with me I wouldn't think twice but I feel I need to tread lightly for his sake at least. God only knows what has happened to him. Anyway, after laying awake half the night, I've decided to go to the bookshop, the one owned by Irshaad's brother-in-law. Maybe I can find out more, or at least get an idea of where Irshaad is hiding.

The brother-in-law's name is Yusuf. I don't tell him who I am; I just walk in like any other visitor. He offers me some tea and shows me the few English language books in the shop. I look through them for a decent amount of time. I want him to think I'm actually looking for a book or magazine or something, don't want to rush it. There are piles of cassette tapes stacked up behind the counter, so on a whim I ask if he has anything by Al Balabil. I need to figure out the best way to say this, need a little time to find my angle. He says he's got a rare tape of one of their live performances, recorded at a private party some years back, so he puts it on and then goes to straighten the magazines on one shelf.

The vocals kick in and I freeze. It's that song, the one that was playing when we stopped near the trees. The soundtrack to my kidnapping.

'Do you know this one?' he asks. He must have seen me react. He doesn't wait for me to answer, just starts telling me about it. He says it's a classic song about *shough il-ghurbah* – the expatriate blues. It's a love story. This couple are separated because he has to leave to work in the oil fields of Qatar or somewhere like that, and she stays behind. Each night they meet in the dream world and write this song together to keep their love alive, and every time he goes to sleep, the man's soul travels further and further away from his body. Yusuf pauses for a moment and then tells me that he's got a theory about it. My heart's racing all of a sudden, like it was when I first came round, my hands tied, blindfolded.

'I'm sorry,' Yusuf says. 'You're obviously tired. You don't need to hear me rattling on about nothing.' He stops the tape. 'My wife's always telling me that I think too much, but what kind of bookseller would I be if I didn't?' He smiles a half smile and pours me some more tea. 'Take as long as you want, all the English books are out here,' he says, and he turns back to the magazine rack.

I pull myself together. 'No, you're right. I do know that song,' I say. He looks up. 'Tell me about your theory.' He pauses for a moment, and then turns back towards me.

'OK. You just listen to it. Listen to the chorus,' he says, and he starts the tape again, holding his finger up to the speaker as they sing.

' "*Your heart shall feel no fear, know no sorrow*." ' A flutter in my throat. That lyric. 'It's written as a love song: 'when we're together my darling your heart shall feel no fear' and so on, but take the window dressing away and what is it?'

I'm just watching him now. I can't move.

'It's a quote from the Koran,' he says. 'It's about justice. "Those who act rightly will have their reward with the Lord. They will feel no fear and know no sorrow." The rebels use it, to strengthen their resolve in the fight for justice. I even heard it in a speech once.'

He leans on the counter. 'I'm not saying that Al Balabil wrote it with that intention, but if they did, they wouldn't be the first artists in Sudan to hide politics in a love song.' He stops for a moment and looks me in the eye. 'Or maybe I'm wrong,' he shrugs. 'I don't suppose it matters, really. In war, all things become tools or weapons.' It's that same line. Yusuf stands back, both hands up now, gesturing along like a schoolteacher as the chorus begins again.

The necklace. I reach down my leg and feel for the string of beads in the zipped pocket; it's not there. Of course it's not there. The dead-eyed man, the JJ, whoever he was, the man in the dark beret, he went on and on about Bilal but not one question about the necklace. They must have taken it while I was unconscious. If what Yusuf says is true, if it was engraved with a rebel slogan, that necklace could have been a message. A warning, or a go order. The rebels' code, and me the unsuccessful messenger.

I pull out my notebook and open the cover. Before we left Geneina I copied out the script, even though it meant nothing to me then. The man's name, and the inscription: there it is, at the top.

I push the book across the counter. 'Is it this?' I ask Yusuf, and he leans over and reads.

'"*For A.Y.Y. Your heart shall feel no fear, know no sorrow*,"' he says, and the song ends.

The shop is silent.

'Where did you see this?' he asks after a long pause, and I take a breath, step back. I look him right in the eye. I need confirmation; I just need to say it.

'Where is Irshaad?'

He stands up straight when I speak, his face flickering briefly with emotion - anger, or doubt, I can't tell. He draws himself up to his full height and places both hands on the counter, either side of my book. I ready myself to run, to move. He stares back at me.

'He's dead,' he says. The words hang in the air between us. I don't say anything, I just wait for him. He looks down and sighs before he goes on. 'He came here to tell me he was going to Chad, a delivery to one of the camps.' The tape squeals and clicks as it switches to the other side. 'The police came to my sister yesterday. They found him just over the border. Bandits. That's what they said.'

The delivery. My bag, my notebook. I open my mouth, about to offer instinctive condolence, but nothing comes out. Irshaad is dead. He must have evaded the kidnappers that day, hid in the trees, then plucked my bag from the bushes. He brought it to me in Chad, my transcripts, everything, and now he is dead. So is Sami, so is Abdulatif. The music starts again. It's the same song, a different version. The party crowd is singing along this time, and as the first chorus begins, all I can hear is Bilal, singing along in the truck as we drove to our kidnapping.

Bilal.

Iva,

I'm sending this now, at the risk of revealing to you the full extent of my recklessness. I can't leave yet. I need to know, for sure. Tomorrow I travel to Zalingei with one of the NGO convoys and from there I hope to find the definitive answer to this. It seems sickeningly clear now, but I need confirmation. I can't think where else he might be. I will try to make contact with the rebels I met, whichever of them might be left, or at least with Abdulatif's family. I should tell them what I know. I owe them that.

The bookshop is my one chance to post this letter, and so before I leave for Zalingei, I will wrap all of these pages together and send them to you. I can't say any more here. I just want to come back with something worthwhile. Take care, sweetheart. I'll be home soon.

Greetings from Darfur

HE BUILT THE CITY long before he arrived, like an ambitious town planner with ideas way above his station. Everything he'd ever heard about it was woven in. His Khartoum was full of broad trees and cool rooms, people of every shade and shape, a skyline of minarets the size of skyscrapers and skyscrapers the size of the sky. There were no laws of physics in his made-up city, nothing to hold him back. The two Niles pumped life into Khartoum like an artery, and he longed to stand at the confluence as soon as he could, to feel it all racing beneath him, seeking the sea.

In the summer of his nineteenth year Daod travelled with a trader convoy to Nyala and then boarded the passenger train that rode east to the capital. The reality of Khartoum was just as elaborate as his imagined city, but it had gravity, and it was loud. The real Khartoum spoke unknown languages in accents that caught in the folds of his ears. It blasted truck horns and music, moved with a rush and urgency that reached from the unpaved streets of the outer suburbs to the centre that stood tall in glass and steel. The rivers split the city like a wishbone; the deep, narrow Blue met the languorous White, then they wrapped around Tuti Island and flowed north together as one. The Great Nile. To the west was Omdurman, the old city, street after street of family compounds and traders stands that stretched out from the sprawling market at the centre. Its edges marched constantly outward with new arrivals, all seeking work. Many of them made the daily crossing east to the industrial landscape of Khartoum North, most productive of the three metropolitan sisters. Long hours in the factories and wide stretches of warehouses, and come evening, or morning, whenever their shift ended, the workers would make their way back across the river to sit in the cafes and cough the remnants of the day from deep inside their chests. To the south, an entirely different commute took place. The White Nile Bridge reached from Omdurman to the financial centre, home to another kind of hustle. Khartoum was where the money was, growing quietly inside sleek buildings that sat cradled like incubation pods between the arms of the two smaller rivers. Daod rode the bus in almost every day and sat near the front, passing change over his head as more passengers squeezed on. Each time the bus crossed the bridge Daod glanced down at the water below to offer a silent greeting.

The bus made its way along leafy Nile Street to the main campus of the University of Khartoum, where the lecture theatres and study rooms became Daod's new home. On lunch breaks, while his classmates debated politics on the lawn, Daod would cross the street to the river's edge. The tourists all faced out, taking photos of the river boats and posing alongside tree trunks or perhaps their rented car. Daod stood with the water at his back and faced the pale brick arches of the Faculty buildings. Elegant lampposts stood sentry along the paths, their lights hanging like droplets that never fell, and behind, the spires of St Matthew's Catholic Cathedral reached up through the canopy. The traffic always slowed when it reached this spot, everyone pausing to look before driving on.

In the time it took Daod to complete his two degrees he made a series of moves from the far edge of Omdurman and a room shared with six factory workers, to within a short walk from the bridge. In the new place, he had his own room, alongside two medical students and one junior barrister. He stopped taking the bus, so that he might walk in and savour that moment when the cool shadows of Nile Street enveloped him.

Daod's barrister housemate was a champion networker, unashamed and charming, and with his introductions, Daod was hired right out of university by one of the biggest practices in the capital. At first he was allowed nowhere near the clients, although he did learn to say 'thank you' and other little phrases in Mandarin. He was the errand boy, essentially: vastly overqualified after law school, but that's how it works for a country lad with no solid connections. He committed himself to his work, entirely, and two years in was made assistant secretary to Mr Hijazi, one of the partners. His wage still barely seemed to cover the ever rising costs of life in the city, but that didn't matter.

There had been years of study and work and at last, his job secure, he felt he could go back home to Kurni for a short visit, knowing for certain that his new life and all he had worked for would be waiting for him upon his return. This time he flew. He spent the journey feeling his way around the contours of his memory. It had been years since he'd been back, and though his mother's bullet point letters had kept him apprised of the more tangible changes, he knew his recollections were slightly stiffened and out of focus. It would be different, and so he tried to prepare. Changes were made, corners knocked off so that it would all fit in, things like his mother's shrinking height, and the village schoolroom, now closed.

Once Daod stepped off the plane in Nyala, the onward journey was slow. He boarded a bus at the edge of the city, and after half a day of stuttered progress, it broke down just past Kass. Daod was still hours from home, and he was forced to catch a ride on the next passing supply truck. The driver had agreed to take him as far as Zalingei, and from there he'd have to figure out the last stretch to Kurni himself. He pulled himself up onto the foot rail and clung to the side, his spare shoes strung to his bag. He was the only man not wearing a jellabiya and headscarf, and thus the only one who wasn't protected from the dust. He improvised with an old work shirt, the collar jutting out over his forehead, the arms wrapped around his chin. Each time the truck stopped to allow smaller, faster vehicles to pass, he peeled one of the shirt sleeves back, blew his nose and then washed his eyes with a little of the water from one of the other men's cans. This happened regularly. Not far from Zalingei they stopped again and this time he swilled the hot water around in his mouth and spat out the gritty contents before taking a swig to swallow. Two aid vehicles passed in the opposite direction, heading out to where the fighting was, or had been. He looked up and caught the eye of the young woman sitting in the backseat of the lead vehicle. She was dressed in a rich blue tobe, bright like the noon sky, and edged in white; he smiled at the ring of fluffy clouds around her face. A Sudanese girl. She looked away. He wondered if his mother would dig a catfish out of the wadi and cook it along with the rest of the food for Eid, and while his thoughts drifted, the dust rose again as the vehicles passed, and the truck moved on.

Most of his old school friends were gone now, probably working away, but the oldest and dearest, Ahmed, was there to meet him. The following day the two of them walked circles round the village together.

'Tell me everything – I want to know about who's doing what. How tall is your little sister now? What did you eat for dinner last night?' He grinned at Ahmed, who happily played along, filling in the details that had been skimmed in the letters from his mother. They could have been the only two in Kurni that day, certainly the only two that Daod noticed. The brightness of the afternoon stretched out before them, and he smiled as his friend detailed all the latest intrigues and blossoming romances. Their wandering brought them to the empty school room. When he'd passed it by last night on his arrival, Daod hadn't even noticed it, caught up as he was in the sweet ease that came with being in the company of an old friend. Today, though, it appeared like a rip in the landscape, nothing but cold open space on the other side. Ahmed lost his job and all of his students four months ago, and though Daod tried writing a letter when he heard, it felt awkward. He didn't know what to say, and so in the end he never sent it.

They approached the gate, and stopped. No getting around this. 'We've started using it again,' said Ahmed, 'for the meetings.' The wind took one corner of the blue metal door and shook it a little, rattling it to check it was closed. The meetings. Daod deliberately hadn't asked about them, wanted to keep it light, just the two of them, grown schoolboys with time for idle gossip and a shared cigarette. He was suddenly aware that the moment was growing as they stood at the hole in the road, weight and expectation piling on. Ahmed brushed his hand down the sleeve of his shirt. The air was so full it could hold no more waiting, surely. Daod opened his mouth in acknowledgement, but before he could speak, Ahmed began. He watched the ground as he spoke, his eyes focussed on some point about three feet below the surface.

'It started with Old Sulayman,' he said. A dispute about his fields, that the herders' camels had overgrazed it, or been allowed on the wrong piece of land, something like that. Angry words and a gun came out, one of the herders shot him in the shoulder, a man that no one recognised. He hit muscle. The next day Sulayman came out into the centre of the village shouting about it all. Said there's no use in contacting the AU, we've called them twice and they still haven't come. They say the weather's too bad, or they've run out of oil. Tell us they're monitoring the situation, that they're aware of it since the fire and theft last year. But what good are nice words when they count for less than dog shit? Sulayman was furious. The herders disappeared and four days later the infection had the old man gripped. He was smaller, like he was shrinking around the wounded shoulder, his anger reduced to a gritty croak. He lay on his bed for almost a week before he died, still mouthing threats at the sky. Daod remembered that from one of his mother's letters: the death, but not the detail.

Ahmed went on; two days later the helicopters flew over, green ones. No guns or anything, not like those seen over the other villages. Just passed over, low and slow. The village men started meeting after that. It was Ahmed's idea to meet in the schoolroom. More space for everyone there, and why not since there were no students in it. He didn't stay for the meetings at first. He just opened it up for them and then made himself busy elsewhere.

Sulayman's son-in-law brought in this military man that his family knew, ex-army from Jebel Marra. The man had deserted and was now with the rebels, one of the splinter groups. The Sudanese Liberation Front. Big guy. Still wore his old uniform with the patches removed. He said he was linked to the group who'd destroyed the government aircraft at El Fasher airbase in 2003. Said he could help with organising.

The meetings took place once a week, a few more men every time. Three weeks went by and the green helicopters continued to fly over. One day, early morning, Ahmed was brushing his teeth and thinking about what to have for breakfast, when he felt it. The ground shook. A deep rumble came through the earth, or through the air, he couldn't tell. Rock shifting on rock, a shivering, and all the chickens in the yard shat and screeched and ran for their roost.

That evening the first of them arrived in town, burnt and horror-struck. People from the bombed out village.

The women took them in, fed and bathed them, and the ones who weren't injured met in the schoolroom. This time Ahmed stayed.

Apparently these villagers said they'd long been having problems with what they thought were bandits – fires, shootings, theft. Once, a woman was kidnapped. Every time they complained to the Governor's office they were fobbed off, told to go home and be good neighbours. Then one morning, they explained, a plane flew over, an Antonov bomber, dropping everything. Another followed. 30 minutes later, men on horseback rode into the fire and cut down anyone who came within their range, swinging machetes, spraying bullets at everything – livestock, people. Janjaweed. A helicopter gunship flew in from the opposite direction and shot people as they fled. Those who survived were the ones who managed to run the right way in that thirty minute gap, find their way to Kurni.

Ahmed said that the next schoolroom meeting was an explosion of anger, everyone talking at once, wanting to know names, tribes, all shouting over each other until the man from Jebel Marra spoke out and everyone fell silent: 'The Arabs don't have planes.' Everyone looked at him. 'Only the government has planes.'

'I didn't speak after that,' Ahmed explained, 'but while they discussed it, my stomach held tight to those words like they were some kind of bad medicine.'

The man from Jebel Marra stood at the front and waved two other men over, gesturing to the large metal crate they brought in at the start. Between them they struggled with the crate, then set it down beside him.

He began to list them all: 'Magabadi. Abota. Agumei. Geri,' and as he did, Ahmed's head emptied. 'Doudata. Um Tissa. Gukar.' Villages. 'Maburikei. Gondo Kria. Ranga. Tolay.' The list went on and on, one after the next, then more, then more, until finally he stopped and let the names settle. 'Destroyed.' He leaned across the crate and opened it. Inside lay a stash of weapons.

'Even from the back,' Ahmed said, 'I could see that these weren't farmer's shotguns. The man from Jebel Marra reached in and started handing the guns to the men at the front of the room. Nobody spoke. They just moved slowly and methodically, turning, passing them back. Karim was in front of me. You know, baker Karim. I stared at the back of his head and like always there was one hair standing out longer than the others, needing to be trimmed. Always that one hair, remember? The antenna. It started obsessing me. I remember sitting behind him as they passed the guns back and all I could think was that I needed some scissors. That hair, it was... anyway, eventually he turned, and we just looked at each other. We sat and stared, the baker and the teacher, the former teacher, eye to eye.'

Ahmed said nothing for a moment, until eventually he looked up at Daod. 'I'll be leaving on Friday, to the training camp.' The question was there in his gaze. A whole conversation in a look – arguments and counterarguments, presentation of the facts, of the slow burial of home, the creeping sand, the shrinking fields, the burning and the fighting coming over the horizon, 70 villages in one short month, nobody listening, nobody stopping it – and in his eyes, the question.

Daod said nothing. A small twister spun around the schoolyard, a whirling dervish, a devotional column of sand.

'I need to get back to Khartoum, my work,' Daod said, and instantly regretted it. He opened his mouth again so that some qualifying phrase could emerge, something to soften it, but nothing came. Ahmed clapped him on the arm, held his eye. He grabbed Daod's hand and pulled him in close, shoulder to shoulder, and as he did, Daod stared past him into the dark of the schoolroom.

Inside the bar at the Grand Hotel the bartender breaks ice into a blender, removes cool glasses from a fridge. On top of the long marble counter sits a small crystal bowl full of limes. 'You're swimming with the big fish now, Daod.' His boss flashes a toothy smile as his staff stand to attention. 'They'll each have another,' Mr. Hijazi says to the bartender, who is already busy making the next drink. 'We're celebrating!' he says, and the bartender nods and hits the button on the blender. Mr Hijazi leans on the bar and raises his voice over the noise. 'We've just secured a big client, one of the international jet set. Lots of elements, UK, Saudi, all the main players.' The bartender keeps nodding occasionally, as if he's listening. He spoons crushed ice into the glasses and smiles benignly as he hands Mr Hijazi a new drink. 'It's going to be a big case,' he says, and he raises his glass even though no one else has one yet. 'Just what we like!'

There's been an accusation of illegal arms trading through Khartoum – guns from Libya, guns to Bosnia, the Chad connection. Government names. The rebels' supporters are trying to bring it to the ICC and link it all to Darfur, to the war and the janjaweed. Mr Hijazi's firm will direct the fight. They will go in hard and say that it's a bald political stunt that threatens the progress of Sudan. They will make it all disappear under a mountain of paper, completely change the view. Daod is a landscape gardener, of sorts.

The bartender finishes pouring the rest of the drinks and slides them to the edge of the bar. They each grab one while Mr Hijazi proposes a toast. 'To the defence!' he says, and everyone holds their glasses high.

Mr Hijazi talks for a while longer about the case, draining the last of his drink, and then he holds the glass up against the light and examines the clumps of ice collected at the bottom. 'You know they make all this from bottled water, right? Only the best!' He presses his other hand against Daod's back. 'Because we don't want you getting sick,' he says, a little too loud. 'You know what they say.' All of the men smile, lean in as he looks right at Daod. 'You're never alone in Darfur, because you've always got a parasite!' They all laugh.

Daod has heard it before. He thinks of the postcards in the hotel lobby, 'Greetings From Sudan' scrawled in stylised script across a collage of pictures of the Meroë pyramids. 'You're Never Alone in Darfur'; he imagines it written in green script, yellow outline, bottom right to top left, reverse for the English version. Four pictures – two wider, two smaller. One of a touk, so typical, rural looking, a perfect thatch, and then one of a man in a jellabiya, an older guy, the wind catching the edge of his scarf as he grins at the camera. His father. Next, his mother, stern faced, composing another clipped letter in her head as she sorts the bundle of grass at her feet. Last picture, smallest, a herd of goats running up a hill, something cliché like that. Off camera to the right is the village schoolhouse. That's where they have the meetings, once a week, with the man from Jebel Marra. Turn over the card and there's space on the back, just enough for a few details, and a name.

'Excuse me please,' Daod tells the men, and he walks out past the restaurant and the patio tables to the changing booths on the terrace. Inside the booth, he removes his trousers, his shirt, one shoe, and then the other. The pool is large and busy. Everyone is otherwise occupied. Daod folds his clothes into a neat pile and then slips out onto the deck. He is in the water before anyone notices.

He presses his back into the wall of blue tile, just out of view of the afternoon sun, and holds his breath. A postcard. He could send a postcard. A few details. A few names, perhaps. A trio of drowned insect bodies rest on the water's surface above, held lightly on the skin of the pool. They turn dizzy circles as a wrinkled foot kicks its way past. His lungs burn, muscles slack. In less than a minute, he will return to the surface and his ears will fill with the shrieking of diplomats' children dive-bombing the deep end, but for now he sits on the bottom, encased, held by water and will and the weight of his body pulling down.

Little Fish

'COME ON, LET'S GO!'

Rayya wobbled as she turned back to the beach, water sucking the sand from beneath her feet. She held one hand over her eyes and licked the sea off her top lip. There he was, sitting just where they'd left him: buried to the hips, the football resting beside the bump of his knees. Osman waved and shouted to them again while little Habib crouched beside him, bum in the air, digging another hole with his small fat hands.

Sulayman threw himself back into the water beside her, kicking as hard as he could, and Rayya closed her eyes against the spray as she reached out, lifted her legs, and swam back to the shore.

It had been a year now since she'd learned to swim, and her two big brothers called her Little Fish. They hardly used her real name anymore. Osman even carved a fish into the head of the bed she shared with Reem, and before she slept each night she traced it with her finger seven times, once for each of them, Mama and Papa too. Back at the house she could only smell the sea, but when night came and she ran her finger across the headboard, she imagined she could hear the tide as it stroked the shore, soothing a restless Gaza to sleep. Rayya heard the gentle roll and shift of the sea as it turned and turned, feeling for the comfy spot in its bed. They sighed and shifted together, Little Fish and the sea, until eventually they drifted into sleep.

It was still dark when she heard the banging. She sat up in bed as her sister's hand clamped down on hers. Someone was at the door.

'No sound,' Reem whispered as she pulled Rayya from the sheets. Whoever had been banging on the front door was now inside, downstairs, shouting things in harsh unfamiliar words. Soldiers. Her sister was up and dragging her to the window. Sulayman pulled Habib behind them.

'Go go, get them out of here,' Sulayman hissed. They were clambering out onto the neighbouring roof when the voices downstairs shouted out a name: 'Osman Ibrahim.'

'GO,' Sulayman said. He didn't follow them, but instead pulled the shutters closed as Reem dragged Habib and Rayya across the rooftop. They jumped down into the neighbour's yard, pushed out through the fence, and ran towards the clump of trees at the end of the alley. As they fled, their brother's name rang out once more on the still night air.

'OSMAN! SULAYMAN!' Mama had been shouting the names of her two oldest sons all morning, one after the next, while Reem held her by the shoulders and shook silently. They were missing. Taken away by the men at the door. Arrested for something, Rayya didn't know what. Maybe taken to the same place they kept her father.

Once her mama's voice had eventually broken from crying, the silence drew in. The house fell still and mute and Reem moved like a ghost around the yard, bringing in milk and eggs, beating out dough, all without making a sound. Rayya cooked the beans, watched as they bubbled and gurgled in the pot, popping with such gentle little breaths that she almost cried at the sound of it.

Soon they'd be going to the police station. Their mama would stand outside, waiting in the long line until someone came out to tell her to go home. Rayya knew all this before it came. Remembered from before, from Papa.

This time, though, she was told to pack her small yellow

bag and go with Reem. They would stop at the market first. Her mama held her for a long time before they left, covered her face in kisses that were still drying by the time they rounded the corner at the end of the road. It wasn't till Uncle Syed greeted them beneath the shade of the market stalls that Rayya realised Reem was not holding a bag of her own. They weren't going to the police station today. They were going somewhere else, and Reem wasn't coming.

After that – after the hiding and the running and the long long trip – Rayya stayed with her aunt and uncle in a small apartment in the midst of Amman's seven hills. From the window of her room she could see the huge Jordanian flag that presided over the valley, and the winking blue eye of the great mosque's dome.   She couldn't smell the sea.

'Your mother will come, with Reem and Habib,' she was told. Her aunt read out the letters that arrived, careful with words like 'be brave' and 'soon'. Rayya began school not long after that, learning to read and write as she waited. It might be a long time before another supply truck crossed the border into Jordan with three empty olive barrels, or maybe a crate hiding half her family. Even longer perhaps till there would be space enough for her lost brothers and Papa too, so she waited with her aunt and uncle, in a city of immigrants, far from home.

Rayya was sixteen when she next saw her little brother. A young man with a wispy beard, Habib sat at their aunt's table that first night, eating bread by the fistful and talking in waves. He too had arrived by truck, hidden in a barrel, and now he crammed the olives into his mouth as he spoke.

'She won't leave. Not as long as they're still in jail.' His fingers were wet with oil. Rayya got up to pour more tea as his words settled.

'And the house? Our room?' she asked. He pinched his slicked fingers together and did not look up. 'No,' he said. 'It's gone.' His eyes sat like tiles in his head, reflecting the light and nothing else. He said it again: 'It's gone.' She felt sick. Stupid. Asking about a bedroom like a spoiled child.

She remembered the bulldozers, their noise as they carried out their unforgiving work several streets away. She remembered their stubborn growl, and what followed: a family shouting in the next street, the neighbours helping to move the broken bricks and pulling out a toy, a pot, a dress. The quiet sounds of fixing.

Rayya wanted her toes to grip the warm sand of the beach once more. She wanted one day on the beach with her brothers, Mediterranean water circling each of their ankles and airborn salt on their skins. She wanted her ears full of those old bedtime songs known only to the sea. A fish carved in wood.

'They're staying with Uncle Syed now,' Habib said, and Rayya said nothing.

★

'Rayya!' The Ward Sister was clicking her fingers above the heads of her busy staff. 'Over here, now!' Rayya moved as quick as the crowd would allow, her arms full of bandages and padding. She'd been back in Gaza for five months now, orthopaedics at Al Shifa hospital, and her work was always needed.

The bombardment started in the night, followed by a firefight in the morning rush hour, grenades on the city streets. Midday came with more referrals from the attacks in Rafah, those who couldn't get across to Egypt. The less critical cases lay in the corridors, waiting for what help was available.

She was good at this. Fast, calm, efficient. She folded bandaging into neat packages around the openings in battered bodies. She moved from one to the next with placid observation, clinical and antiseptic, applying just enough time to each, no more. Secure the injured limb, stop the bleeding, clean the wound, keep moving.

She'd been at home when it had started, drifting gently between sleep and wake. Her mother's snores were keeping a steady pace while Reem's slow footsteps marked the path between kitchen and hall in insomniac rhythm. The rumble of the blast shook Rayya awake, and within minutes she was up, dressing herself, and then picking her way through the dark streets to Al Shifa. That was about nine hours ago.

The stream of injured people had peaked just after one, and the noise in the clinic was cacophonous. Rayya felt some comfort at being part of it, at being central and active, and it was only on the Sister's firm instruction that she took the tea she was offered and sat for a moment of rest on the back step. Outside, the street was full. It was the same every time; once the fighting died down, everyone would line up at the door of the nearest bakery, the grocery store, buying as much as they could afford in case this time it was the start of something larger.

Habib had been and gone twice already – once to confirm that Mama and Reem were fine, and a second time to bring food for the staff. Habib was serious and kind, had grown into a man who spoke little and thought lots. Since Rayya and he returned together from Amman, he busied himself every day at the clinic, or at the homes of their extended family. He was Rayya's closest age-mate, and after the years in Amman, her closest soul-mate too.

She found that her childhood memories bore little relation to where she lived now. Her memories were pinned on to people, on to old phrases and songs, but not to the physical structures of the place – the streets, the buildings. The fish on her bed was long gone. She remembered lighting matches as a child whenever bad things happened, thinking the soldiers would run from the flame like frightened animals. Now she held up first aid kits and antibiotics.

The work was important, a way of bringing her Jordanian education home to her battered city, but more than that it supported her family. She brought in almost enough money to cover the food and rent. With the little extra that Habib and Reem made here and there, they could survive, but she knew with a bigger salary they could actually save money, perhaps rebuild their family home. When she was offered a well-paid job with an international NGO, she didn't think long before she accepted.

*

Sudan had a familiar feel to it, Geneina in particular, despite it being further inland than she could ever have imagined. It was the busy streets, even though they were full of donkeys and made of sand, more like an old-fashioned rural village than a state capital.

She walked the twenty minutes from residence to office compound every morning at 7am. The truck came half an hour later to ferry her and her colleagues to work, but she preferred the dawn walk. The sand was still cold from the night as it tumbled over sandal sides and edged its way under her feet. She had twenty minutes at the start of each day to smell the bakery's first offering and trace the white tendrils of morning fires against the waking sky.

'It's a security risk. You need to come in the vehicle with us,' she was told, at first. 'It's for your own safety,' Antonia said, and then after a long conversation, 'I understand.' Once she'd told them about the moving, the running, and the bulldozed house, they stopped trying to contain her. They let her walk. One magic word – Palestine – and they all fell silent.

Rayya travelled out from Geneina to Mornei Camp every two weeks to assess the health programmes and deliver the wages. Always in convoy, they drove the same winding tracks back and forth till she began to know each bush, wadi crossing and hairpin bend.

Today was payday. She sat in the front passenger seat with the bag of bundled money on the seat behind, next to her chattering assistant, Najah.

'So if we stay for one night this time we might not be able to do the supervision interviews with all the health promoters tomorrow. We need to leave by 2pm, so I've drawn up a list of those who we need to speak to most urgently.' Najah began rattling off names like an auctioneer. Asad hummed as he drove, providing a quiet accompaniment to Najah's staccato pronouncements.

'I spoke to the cook on the radio as well – told her to have food ready for our arrival...' and on and on. Rayya stared ahead and let her peripheral vision embrace the horizon as they drove up out of a tangle of bushes and onto an open plateau.

'Rayya?' Her name had been repeated more than once before she heard it and responded. 'Did you smoke shisha in Amman? In the coffee shops?'

Najah's favourite subject: Amman. Without waiting for an answer, she continued:

'In Khartoum, some women smoke in public places, so my cousin says. But it's not really accepted.' She looked over at an impassive Asad with delighted eyes, wanting his response and getting none. 'So, in Amman, is it acceptable for women to smoke in public? Maybe rich, sophisticated women? Foreign women definitely. Old women too, perhaps? Or any women?' Najah would go on like this, firing out questions until she'd covered every angle of the issue, at which point she'd fall silent and wait as Rayya tried to answer as many of the questions as she could remember. Smoking in Amman. They hadn't covered this one before.

'I've decided I'm going to start smoking.' Rayya still hadn't answered. 'My aunt smokes, outside her kitchen, in the back.' Over the last few months they had discussed Amman's weather, shopping, style of buildings, popular music, political system and general statistics (population, elevation, rates of employment and crime). Also, schooling for girls, tribal composition, local customs with regard to hospitality towards strangers, layout and locations of largest markets, and cost of accommodation in the old town.

'What's your favourite flavour of tobacco?'

'Apple,' Rayya replied without needing to think, and with the word still in her mouth she saw the head of the first horse as it emerged from the bush.

Next was its rider, sitting high in the saddle, rifle to the sky. Then came another, and another. More of them kept appearing – five, six, seven – sealing the road both forwards and back. Janjaweed. Asad slammed his foot to the brake pedal and Najah choked back a cry. Rayya did not move.

The men were shouting, blazing with anger. One made his horse rear up on its hind legs. He stood tall in the stirrups and fired a round above the roof of the vehicle. Another man jumped down off his horse and strode towards them, gun raised. He looked from Asad to Rayya, then moved to her passenger window, screaming through the glass, 'Open it, open it bitch! Open the window!'

No one else spoke. Rayya did not look up. She kept her eyes on the dip in the man's throat – the hollow that collected sweat and dirt and moved with each breath he drew. The hollow contracted once more – 'Open the fucking window, bitch!' Rayya's hand was at the door, scrabbling for the window handle. 'The money – give us the money.' They knew.

'Najah,' Rayya called to her in a low flat voice. 'The bag.' She held her hand between the seats, feeling for the straps. Najah lifted the bag from beside her and pushed it between the two front seats. The man was now screaming like a psychotic market seller, repeating the same phrase again and again: 'Giveittomegiveittomegiveittome.' The straps on the bag were tangling, twisting as they pushed it towards him, catching on the gear stick, then Rayya's scarf.

'Nownownow!' he screamed, and at last the bag tipped through the open window and landed with a thump on the ground outside. The janjaweed clicked his fingers for another of the men to fetch it. The hollow at the base of his throat was fluttering, pulsating. Rayya willed him away with silent concentration.

'Look at me – look at me, khawaji bitch,' he bellowed. 'Look.' She lifted her eyes and saw only the open end of his rifle as he brought it up to her face. Right between each closing eye, the cold metal pushed against her forehead, burning a mark, trying to read the inside of her head. Rayya was cool, blank. Her mind was a fresh hospital sheet, still as a sterile bandage. This was not the first time she'd had a gun in her face. She shut her eyes and breathed desert air and screaming, bulldozers and olive crates, 'Where are you from, khawaji bitch?' – one long continuous stretch of water and sky; she breathed out.

The crack of the gun was so loud, her ear must have burst.

'Move, move, move!'

She couldn't feel it, not yet. Couldn't feel the pierce or the shatter.

Rayya opened her eyes. Another deafening shot. The militia man laughed, smashed the butt of his rifle down onto the roof of the vehicle, then turned away and ran. He was up onto his horse, smiling, sweeping his weapon past them in one final arc before he turned and followed the rest of his band back into the bush.

Najah began to pray out loud from the back seat, crying and begging, thanking and sobbing as Asad started the engine, pulled a jerky U turn at the widest point of the road, and then sped back to base.

Rayya hadn't spoken to anyone since she'd given the statement three days ago. Not really. Just hello, thank you. She slept little and lightly. Pots of food and tea appeared by the door of her room, but no one pushed for more. All of her words were written down in her statement and each of the documents Antonia had produced from it: the incident report, the staff health assessment, the highlighted section in the interagency security briefing.

The time alone had given her the opportunity to catch up on her work, to climb the mounds of paper that grew every time she looked away. Without the distraction of conversation she could work much faster, completing reports and evaluations deep into the night.

Just after midnight, Rayya walked out of her room and into the yard with her eyes down, trying to remember where she'd left the other laptop lead. The generator would stay on while the others were still up, so she might as well make use of it to charge the spare battery. She should be able to work through till three at least if she could get that second battery charged up.

'She won't talk about it,' she heard Antonia say as she rounded the corner into the main courtyard. The words whipped up little dust storms that spun and twisted through the compound. She scuffed her foot on a stone as she stopped, and all of them turned to her, their eyes wide with concern. They'd been trying to force rest on her. Trying to make her stop the work. But what else was she here for, if not for work?

'I'm fine,' she told them earlier when they asked how she was feeling, asked if it had 'hit' her yet. Fine. She was fine.

Rayya pulled her scarf tight, fixing her hijab and tucking her thick hair behind her ear once more. The air smelt of diesel. Her throat began to swell again, as if something were growing in it.

She looked at the ground, felt the pull of the laptop and the mountain of files she'd had moved in from her office, and the thing in her throat grew bigger. It was swelling down into her chest, tight fingers reaching for her lungs, her heart.

Rayya pulled at the scarf she'd tightened only moments ago, and gasped for breath. A bulldozer was parked on her chest. Come to dig out the foundations she had hidden below, foundations she laid down years ago in the bottom of an olive crate. Her legs pushed her out into the light of the courtyard, treacherous muscles marching her away from the safety of her room.

Antonia caught her as she pitched forwards, lowering her into a chair, pulling loose the scarf that hung from her neck. Antonia was talking, garbling questions and busy hands.

'Rayya! Rayya! Look at me.' Rayya's head was being moved, fingers cool on the sides of her face. Beneath, the digger bore down, dug its teeth into flesh, pressed its metal tread against ribs, crushing her insides.

'I – my heart – my –,' Rayya clutched at her chest, clawing her clothes with one hand while the other hung stiff and useless at her side. Where was Habib? He'd know what to do, how to help. Strong enough to stand in for three missing men, little Habib. Strong enough, just as Rayya was strong enough. Two giants disguised as fish, sly slippery creatures, nimble and clever, seeking shelter in the tiniest of crevices and overhangs. They always moved fast enough to keep ahead of the current.

The vice grip closed around her, pulled her into places where the water was heavy. Pulled her in. Was this a drowning? A drowning on dry land, suffocated by the thick hand of the Darfur air. She opened her mouth wide. Wider. Almost broke her own jaw with trying, and as she felt herself being laid out flat, flopping and heaving on the ground, gasping, eyes rolling back inside her head, she heard a voice declare, 'This is a panic attack. Rayya, do you hear me? You are going to be OK.'

Her head was held from below and as she slipped under, beneath the seam of the sky and the sea, she clenched her fist tight and forgot, completely, how to swim.

Jebel Moon

THE NIGHT IS CALM and cool and I wake just before dawn, Hussein still snoring in the shelter beside me. If we were any closer to one of the villages, I'd have insisted on someone keeping watch all night, but out here, away from the roads, there's no need. No one's coming. I walk down a little way from the shelter for my morning piss. The sun is breaching the horizon, so after, I smoke a cigarette and watch it climb. A wall of red dust approaches from the north, half a mile high, moving fast, and the sun is still cut in half by the land when the dust storm reaches us. Before heading back to the shelter to wait it out, I pull my scarf up over my face and lean hard into the wind, watch through squinted eyes as the earth obliterates the sky.

An hour later the storm breaks and so does our scout camp of two. We follow the curve of the wadi bed, the bloodless vein that runs south to Kurni. We approach from behind a rise of rock and get down on our bellies, crawl up to the ridge and count heads in the camp below. There are more of them here now, and far more dwellings than I remember, but most of these aren't homes, not real ones. The original village is a thin drawing buried beneath the new camp, barely an outline now: the main road, the sheikh's compound, the schoolhouse, all overrun with outsiders, newcomers who've attached themselves and sucked it dry, covered it in shitty little tents made of sticks, plastic sheeting slapping at the air. An hour and we've got a rough headcount, about five hundred, plus the original villagers. They have some animals with them – a small herd of cattle, some horses and a few camels. No foreign water system put up by the khawajis, though there is a drilling rig and truck on the far side. Doesn't look like they've done any work yet, so for now there's just one lonely well. The sun hits that angle, the one that says it's almost time to find shade and eat fatur, so we crawl back down the ridge and head north to where our horses are tethered at the clump of tree stumps. They're dehydrated and we need them fit for the next manoeuvre, so we decide to take them by the reins and walk them to the abandoned police hut a few miles out. We wait in the shade till midday is past, and then ride back to base.

I don't mind the walking. Some of the young lads, they're keen for action but they can't hack the walking. Not me. I trained with the best. Two years in Libya, and before that four in the government corps. Months spent in a pastel green uniform, marching in and out of the desert. Humans are like dogs in that respect: that urge to walk, the pull of the horizon. It's part of our blood and our sinew. Back at base, I say this to one of the young guys from Chad and he gets aggressive, starts shouting, 'Are you saying we're dogs? That God's people are dogs?' Wilfully stupid, these boys. 'No. That's not what I –' 'Are you saying –' on and on until I clip him with the back of my hand. So quick to start shouting dogma, these kids and their half-learned holy anger. They soon drop it. Later on, when I spot a dog scrounging around the edge of the base, I watch it through the sight on my rifle for a while before letting it run away.

There's a lot of waiting. A lot. That's another thing the kids don't like. I use the time to think, oil the seams of my boots, check my equipment, practice runs in my head. They've got our intel on the village, and while I'm sure of what happens next, I don't say anything. My job is observation, and readiness. The orders come from regional command and until we get word, we wait.

We're finally called in for the briefing and I draw out the plan on the ground. We'll wait for the bombers to pass and then follow in on horseback, camel and truck. Four SAF jeeps arrived this morning, and they'll drive to the camp perimeter, a few hundred meters out, just to make sure we keep it contained, keep the zurgas near the centre so we're not chasing in every direction like last time. The Army guys tend to hang back and let us do the work, which is fine by me.

We've got a few hours till we go, so we check over our horses again, make sure they drink. Mine has a bad tooth, looks like it's going rotten, so I make a note to pull it once this raid is over. We check our rifles, stash extra rounds on our belts and in the horses' panniers, and then eat a little food.

I look over the map I drew in the ground and add a few extra details, make it more like how it was before. I must have been ten, that first time. There were more trees. The edge of the desert was a lot further north then, nowhere near the village. Fewer people but more fields, much better grazing. It was a four week ride with my father and his men, me on my first big trading trip, en route to the Zalingei market and then back through Geneina to the border and our family out west, in Chad, before we went home to Jebel Moon. I rode behind him, sat tall, felt like a man for the first time, chin up in all but the strongest of winds. We didn't stay here long. Stopped off in the village while my father negotiated a few sales, took in some of their goods and sold spice, a few cloths. He didn't know the sheikh that well as we usually took the routes further north, but we traded with them a few times. The village was more defined then, with muscular trees along the wadi, tough crops that stretched out north, not like now with the sand slowly devouring every decent grazing place, choking off life and turning the world still and sterile. Harder to navigate too, for anyone who likes landmarks.

Me, I was taught the night sky. Hours awake and looking up from the south face of our mountain, my grandfather pointing out each formation and the relationships between distant glimmers of light and the setting point of the sun. Al-Sufi's lessons, he called them, all hung from the back of a bear. By the time I was fifteen I could find my way over most of the northern state by night. Look for the spaces between the light, that's what he taught me. The stars don't mean anything without the dark, and up there, everything stays the same.

When the orders come down, we move fast. Riders to our horses, more in the jeeps. Unit One departs as the Antonovs pass overhead. Thirty minutes later, Unit Two follows. We ride out of the base, army escort just visible to the west. My head empties. From here until sundown it will be blood rushing in my ears and the beat of horse's hooves. I won't feel the burn of sore muscles till tomorrow.

We ride into the camp behind the trucks and everything speeds up. The Army boys pull out to the edges of the encampment. Unit One have the herd. A small group of them lead the animals out into the bush, make sure none of them get loose. The zurgas run everywhere, chaotic zig zags, screaming to each other, trying to carry things. Looks like the khawajis took off in their truck. Their rig stands alone at the edge. We'll get that later. The wind picks up and the flames leap from the shacks on the outskirts and rush towards the centre of the village. Gunfire.

Hussein is ahead of me and there, off to the left, they're filling the well, the voices echoing off the sides, shrill like the horses. I close my ears and look for the gap. To my right, an open space between two sagging tents not yet eaten by fire, and there it is in the stillness, my target, grabbing for something. I move to face it, grip my horse tight between my legs and rise a little in the saddle. There. It is panicking, looking for something, I don't see what – I just see the pause, that split second of indecision as I lower my barrel, powder, pressure, case, the tight skin of its forehead one small point in a yawning sky and I breathe out, squeeze.

I lean left and turn as she falls to her knees, hands empty, in the dirt behind me.

The Waiting Room

WHAT I REMEMBER IS this: summers so short and hot the grass barely had a chance. Running down to the Red River and the new roads beyond, winter salt still staining them pale grey. The two of us lying beneath a sprinkler, shirtless, with no hassle from anyone, our eyes squeezed shut against the sky.

I remember the wood frame skeletons of the new houses, a whole load of them sitting in crescents by the dike, making postcards of the sun as it set late and shone through homes so new they didn't even have skin on them yet. I remember making our own worlds in those houses, racing up and down the stairs, shrieking as the bats came in at last light, sitting for hours with the orange cat as she licked her pile of newborn kittens.

One of the skeleton houses had a pool out back, a huge hole with no tiles yet, just pure smooth concrete. We threw in an old armchair that we dragged from the dumpster, doused it with lighter fluid and screamed with delight as it burned. Dizzy. Blew black stuff out of our noses the next day, but told no one. A secret. A beautiful black-snot secret.

Now in Darfur, I get the same smell: a bottle full of burning gasoline flies over the wall in the night, explodes on the ground and takes out two plastic garden chairs and a ropey banana tree. It's the same feeling I had that night with the armchair, but it's all wrong this time, the wrong reaction in the wrong place, so I feel it, and keep it to myself. Everyone else is gasping, or shouting, or running to the street to see who could have thrown it. I just stand there in the dark watching it all, watching the smoke turn out the stars.

We open up at 8.30 every morning, 9.30 on Fridays, and every day there's a line. I say hello on the way in, greet the regulars, our repeat visitors, and thank everyone for being patient. I open up the consulting rooms, the waiting room, and then unlock the main gate. We've got four community nurses now, so they run the triage. Our senior trauma nurse arrives from Palestine in two weeks, and once she's here we'll be able to properly set up the satellite clinic in Mornei. Until then, we run a basic service. I do more and more of the paperwork, less face to face, but Fridays I take the front with Joan, the nurse from South Sudan.

Joan makes a pot of wickedly strong coffee, and we open up. Today is slow, Friday before Eid, but there's Samia and her little boy again, sitting in the shade of the waiting room, wiggling her toes in orange flip flops. She's been in every few days for the last week or so, first for dehydration treatment and worming for the boy, then for supplemental nutrition. That's our thing: basic medical intervention, simple procedures. The idea is that people don't have to leave the camp if all they need is rehydration salts, basic wound sterilisation and dressings. We administer injections, monitor weights, peer into eyes, ears and mouths. When anything complicated shows up we make a referral to the clinic in town where the doctors have surgical instruments and high end drugs and a whole lot less sand in their waiting room.

Samia knows all this. She sits beside another regular, Maha, an old woman who told me she got her name because her eyes were as big as a cow's. Maha squints through stubby lashes, those big cow eyes half-hidden behind heavy lids. She looks regal, high cheekbones and a broad forehead. She must have been a stunner.

The first time she came in, her daughter-in-law was holding the severed end of Maha's pinky finger in a scrap of cloth. Maha cuts herself. Every time she loses a family member to the violence, she chops the end off one of her fingers with a butcher's cleaver. This we managed to get out of the daughter-in-law, once she'd calmed down. Right now Maha has two intact thumbs, and one index finger. On that first visit she was bleeding really bad, faint and almost unable to walk. We managed to staunch it, get some stitches in. The finger stub wasn't so lucky.

She came back to get the stitches out the following week and has been visiting us since then, coming in to talk with Joan mostly. She waits for the quieter times, Fridays, and corners Joan with questions. The discussion goes on for weeks, with Maha interviewing Joan on every aspect of the struggle in South Sudan. Christian, mostly, but still having to fight the government for their rights, having to fight for recognition, just like here. Maha wants details. She wants to know how these things play out, how they might end.

'Joan will be free soon,' I tell her as I pass through, and she acknowledges me with a serious nod.

Samia's toes have stopped wriggling in the flip flops. I gesture for her and she rises slowly from her seat, follows me to the consulting room. I weigh the baby again, check his ears. Abdul Waheed. He's tiny. Not really a baby in age, he's over two years old now, but he's confined to Samia's back most of the time, too weak to walk much.

Last time she was in she told me his father is janjaweed.

'And you?' I ask her through the translator. 'Can I examine you too?' She smiles a little and opens her hands. I check eyes, ears, mouth. Heartbeat, breath. She's lost a lot of weight. Could be malnutrition, or just an immune system depressed from the chronic insomnia that everyone suffers. White spots in her mouth, swollen glands. Could be a number of things.

'I'd like to take some blood for testing,' I say, and she shrugs, smiles again and agrees. I get out a 20 gauge needle and a handful of vials as Abdul Waheed sighs a baby snore on the table beside his mother.

The winter after we burnt the armchair you met Wyatt. I laughed at his name and his haircut, the Nodak mullet, straight off the farm. Twenty below in Fargo and us like trapped rats, so we drank rum in his basement, looking for whatever we thought might get us high: whip-its, nutmeg, squeezing each others' necks until we passed out and slid down the wall, came back up with the head spins. A long way till the melt.

Wyatt was king of the good times, a constant supply of things to make us laugh till our bellies hurt, him content to sit back and watch as we went into orbit. So we did. You led the way, one night leaping from the top of the tire swing into a bank of snow so big you couldn't get out for laughing. You gave up after a while and just lay there. I ended up digging you out with a garbage can lid, my hands so cold I thought my fingers would snap off.

It wasn't long till Wyatt started tying tubing around your arm, one syringe between us. You got quiet, and I did too.

It didn't show up for years. Not till we'd all but forgotten about sliding down basement walls and torching old furniture in rich people's pools. All that was a lifetime away.

Incubation was what the doctors called it. Made me think of hibernation, of a cave in the snow, pure white walls and muffled sound, you needing nothing more than a winter of deep sleep and to wake in the spring, refreshed.

Once it came on it was vicious. This was before cocktails and viral loads and long life expectancy, this was back in the days of counting T cells and saying your goodbyes long before you were ready. Your parents were hysterical, and Wyatt was nowhere to be found. Possibly dead already.

We met a few times after my test came back and we tried not to pinpoint it, tried to avoid looking for the moment when infected blood came for you and not me.

I held two words behind my teeth for that whole year. Kept them from coming out, from hitting you like a useless sack of sympathy and too damn late. I'm sorry, and that amounts to exactly nothing.

I've told Samia that I'm sending her samples off for testing, and that we're looking for hepatitis and glandular fever. I haven't told her we're also looking for HIV.

There's no provision for it, officially. Officially, it does not exist. Not in Sudan. Not in Darfur.

Samia's blood will be the fourth I've sent for testing this month, and there will be more. More people who are officially healthy, their deaths explained as 'cause unknown'. It's not in any of the budget lines, but I see it here in the consulting rooms, along with rape babies and girls with brutal scarring between their thighs. Here's what doesn't get counted in the official statistics, sitting in our plastic chairs, waiting for antibacterial wipes and painkillers.

Samia scoops Abdul Waheed into the papoose cloth and binds him close to her, covering his head with the loose end before heading back out into the late morning sun.

In the waiting room, Maha and Joan drink coffee.

'Now this one, this one didn't even hurt,' Maha says to Joan. She holds her hands off her lap, spreads the stubs of her fingers. She speaks for a minute in Arabic and then finishes in English. 'I'm too old to be scared,' she says, and she presses her lips together, toothless and defiant.

We and the Moon are Neighbours

WE WORK ON THE edge of town, in a lot that Khadija's brother found for us. Well, it's the edge of town now. Geneina's grown rapidly in the last few years but the ground out here is too rocky to build on. It falls away in a small cliff, down through a mess of boulders to our lot and then the road that runs north, so there's no chance of us being pushed out by anyone looking to build a new house here. There are a few trees for shade, and the small wadi runs nearby, underground. We reach the water by digging. The perfect spot for making pots.

Today we are sifting through soil to prepare it for moulding. As we work, Talah pounds grain for tomorrow's meal, singing quietly to the beat of her stick – 'We and the Moon Are Neighbours', her favourite since she was young. Her uncle brought some cassette tapes back from Khartoum a few months ago and one of them was a compilation of Fairouz. She hadn't heard it for years, not since the last tape broke, so she's been playing this one as often as she can, and while we're at work she continues acapella. It would usually be two of them on the same bowl of grain, working it in time like horses' hooves, but with the others away she's got twice the work. She keeps the beat moving fast, and the rest of us hum along with her. Small things to help with the repetition.

By the time we stop for breakfast my back is aching and she's pounded a bowl of grain to flour. Talah has been tending the fire since early morning, bringing the coals back down to a deep red glow for cooking. She brings us small glasses of hot sweet tea, and flatbread emerges from a length of cloth. We eat it with the beans from yesterday, and sit beneath the trees. I lean back into the broad trunk behind me and close my eyes. Rest. Take a sip of tea and let sweetness fill my throat.

'Talah!' Khadija calls to her daughter as she pokes at the coals on the stove. 'Where are you girl? The beans are burning!'

Talah jolts into action, wide-eyed and apologetic. She is sixteen now, but her mother still holds off the suitors.

'I won't have her trade herself to the first man who arrives with big promises and lusty eyes,' Khadija told us once. 'We make our money here.' She'd made this declaration one day after Talah was followed home by a loud and pushy man looking to make her his wife. 'These old men,' Khadija spat, 'they think they can buy anything they see – the onion seller as well as the onions.'

We watched the whole thing from the corner: he waited until Talah was on her way back from the market, then caught her, blocking her way and demanding attention. She lowered her eyes and began to greet him in the long and complicated manner appropriate to his seniority. She spared no flourish. She remembered to enquire about his family, each wife subtly acknowledged as she asked after their health in the most respectful tones. She was searching through the names of each daughter when Khadija came waddling round the second bend in the road. 'Talah! Move it!' she shouted, pretending not to see the old man so she could really bellow, throw the weight of her voice without giving cause for offence.

He turned at the sound of her. His back sagged a little and he stepped away from Talah who, offering eloquent goodbyes, moved towards her mother. Khadija stood with her hands on her hips, the muscle of her lower arms dusted with dry clay and sweat. 'Back to the market old man,' she muttered, and he turned and made an obedient retreat.

The rest of us watched at the corner as if it were a game of football, our tobes held across our mouths to hide our laughter.

Now the beans settle inside me, a warmth resting at my centre. I shut my eyes as I listen to the gossip. '…and now she sends her sons to El Fasher to study, to live with her brother. With what money I don't know.'

Fahima, Miriam's sister-in-law. The one nobody speaks to, according to Miriam anyway. 'She's working for one of the NGOs,' says Miriam evenly, 'in an office.'

The others cluck their tongues and say nothing.

The only other sound at this mid-point of the day is the wind, and the gentle crackle of the coals on the stove. Talah pours more tea.

'Maybe they'll buy some pots.' Khadija's sharp voice cuts into the silence.

'What?'

'The NGO. Maybe they will buy pots from us. Miriam…'

Miriam is shaking her head, turning her hands over and fussing with the folds of her tobe.

'Miriam, you should speak to Fahima, tell her we can make them to order, whatever size or design they want. Food storage, water. You know they ship fridges in from Khartoum? Tiny things that need a generator running all night just to keep one little block of cheese cool. They've got lots of money, these NGOs.' Miriam waves a dismissive hand and looks away, but Khadija keeps on. 'I heard that they pay their watchmen more than a doctor's wage.'

'That's not true.'

'It is. Salim told me. They've got those huge TVs as well. Gas stoves, air conditioners…'

'Fine! So why would they want our pots then?!' Miriam is on her feet, pacing. The end of her tobe slips from her shoulders as she turns and beneath, her dust streaked t-shirt clings to patches of sweat on her body.

'You could talk to her.'

'I can't talk to her. I won't. She isn't the family cow for us to milk. Don't ask me again. Just – no!'

One of a wandering herd of nearby goats leaps through the broken bits of what Talah calls the pot graveyard. It bleats at us, tongue out, laughing. It seems to surprise itself with its daring and stands for a brief moment before running back to join its sisters as they pick through the rubbish in the wadi.

The moment has broken, and with even Khadija holding her tongue, we move to the piles of fine sand and soil that still need mixing.

Clumps of earth crumble between my fingers as I work through the plate in front of me. I am red to the knuckles, stained by soil. I can feel the skin tightening and know I'll need to oil my hands before I sleep tonight.

Talah is making more tea. Water begins to simmer in the pan and she hums the same song again.

'Talah – that singing voice might catch you a prince one day,' I say.

She looks up at me and smiles at my teasing.

'No need for a do-nothing man who wants you only so he can brag to his friends about his new virgin,' Khadija shouts. She has always been straight to the bone with her words. Talah, for her part, works hard making pots as well as our food and drink. As long as she's here with us, and we sell what we make, she can wait for her husband. We haven't been selling as much as we used to for a while now, but we don't talk about it, don't talk about what that might mean.

I smile back at Talah and she looks down, stirs the water.

I see Asif crouched there in front of the tea. He sees me and he leans towards me. Traces of his smell work their way through me still. My eyes focus on the sand in my hand and I imagine him sitting with me, behind me, hand on my back where the shade of the tree has slipped and the sun is now holding me. Thirteen months and no word from him yet.

Talah speaks my name again, standing over me with tea. I take a glass and sip, rise from my plate of clay. I stretch up and let my vertebrae crunch back into position.

The road stretches out into the flat of the plain and at the far end, a wedge of dust rises. The African Union soldiers live halfway to the airport, in neat rows of large square tents that stand out against the pale ground like fired bricks.

In the IDP camp in Ardamata, not far from the AU base, the tents are smaller, family size, and bright white with UN logos splashed in blue along the sides. More temporary homes every day.

The home Asif and I built is still strong, with sturdy walls that I patched myself, pushing mortar between each big brick, fingers stiff as the drying earth. Asif hired some men to help him with the thatch, and the first night we spent under it we were soaked in the deep damp smell of fresh grass. For a few weeks the smell lingered, even when the roof dried hard, and now each collection of animal feed has me breathing in and holding the lush weight of that memory in my chest.

I'm swirling the last drops of tea around my glass when a jeep squeals to a halt at the bottom of the slope. A train of dust catches up with the vehicle and wraps around it as two people climb out and approach us. I recognise the small neat step of Salim immediately. He has worked at almost every stand in the market and now he drives for the NGO.

He picks his way deliberately, delicately. He never did lose the grace of his youth. He smiles as he approaches. With him walks a woman, tall, wrapped in the night sky blue of a Khartoum woman: businesslike. Her face is covered against the dust from the jeep and she is almost right in front of me before I realise who she is.

'Salaamu'alikum.'

'Wa'alaikumsalaam.' I slip the empty glass into my pocket.

'It's lovely to see you, Aisha. How are you? How is your health?' She is discreet, doesn't ask after Asif.

'Very…very well, thank you. And you?' I ask. 'How are you and your family?'

Miriam is turning, hearing, seeing.

'They are all very well, thank you for asking.'

Miriam stands staring for a moment, then takes one step away. Khadija catches her arm and whispers something into the drape of fabric around Miriam's face. Whatever she says seems to stop Miriam from leaving, but she stands taut like the skin of a drum.

The dust cloud has passed and so Fahima allows her tobe to drop a little looser around her shoulders, revealing her whole face. She turns to Miriam. Salim coughs, runs his fingers across his moustache. 'Salaamu'alikum,' he says softly, quickly. His eyes jump between us.

We are mere spectators as Fahima and Miriam wait for the whistle. They greet one another with stiff precision, and then pause.

Fahima speaks first. 'My organisation is working in Geneina with the people now living in Ardamata Camp and some of others – providing them with clothing, blankets, medical assistance and so on.' She speaks in plurals, in masculine. 'We are also training them in how to – how to wash properly and not get ill from dirty food.' Her language slips a little as her eyes flick over our cooking pots, our buckets of water, our work-worn hands. Miriam stiffens further and shifts her weight as Salim deploys another cough, followed by a quick smile that he fans round at each of us in turn.

'Have you come to teach us how to wash, Fahima?' Miriam lifts her chin, sucks air between her teeth. Behind her, Talah responds by pulling her tobe low across her face, wrapping it round till only her eyelashes are visible. Khadija hovers near Miriam, and I do not move. The goats bleat out an excited chorus.

I expect to see the spark between them catch light in Fahima's mouth, but instead she is calm. 'I've come to ask for your help.'

Miriam's laugh falls out like a stone, just one, and Fahima continues. 'They need a steady source of clean water. Some of them have been here for two years now, and there are already too many people for the few good wells that are left. They can't go back to their villages. Some have been burnt to the ground more than once, so this might be their permanent home now. One of the other NGOs is planning to drill new boreholes, but –'

'Yes, yes, and what can we do? We don't get paid in foreign wages. We work fourteen hours every day just to keep ourselves afloat. We pray for every one of those people in your camps and we keep our heads down when the janjaweed ride along this road at night,' her voice getting louder, 'and then we let our sons and our husbands leave to fight them.' My stomach twists at this. 'Now you want our help? You?' She leans on one hip, daring Fahima to speak. 'How long did you practice your speech for me?'

Khadija is moving forward, her hand at Miriam's elbow again.

'What do you want here?' Her voice lifts, floating like an open hand in the air.

Fahima blinks and swallows. I shift to my other foot, watch the two of them while Talah busies herself with the cooking pots behind us, working quietly.

'I'm here with an offer.' Fahima speaks at last. 'We want them to have their own method of obtaining clean water. A filter, something they can afford. We have a man working

81

with us now, from South America, a potter like you. He knows how to make simple filters, the same style as your pots. He can show you, teach you to make them.'

She pauses. Finding no interruption except the sharp rise of Miriam's eyebrow, she goes on. 'My organisation will buy the first order from you, maybe forty or fifty of them, and then you can sell more to the other NGOs when they see how good this is. You can also sell to ordinary customers in Geneina – a higher price for those with decorative designs, whatever you want…'

'Yes yes,' Khadija cuts in, not wanting to be outdone by Fahima's business talk. 'How much will you pay us for them? And what does this man want? Who pays his salary?'

'I – my organisation will pay him to teach you the method, and buy the mould you will need, as well as the silver compound to coat the inside and make the pots into filters. He says it's very simple.'

I imagine a thin bangle of silver pressed into clay, a pot glowing pale as if the moon was held within. Fahima continues.

'You already have everything else you need. You can sell at a price that is good for you, higher than what you're making now, but it will be low enough for ordinary people. Every household in Geneina will want one.'

Fahima takes a pencil and business card from her purse, and writes something across the top. She holds it out, and for a moment nobody moves. Khadija eventually reaches up and takes the card, slides it into her pocket.

Fahima hitches her purse back up onto her shoulder and tugs at her clothing, arranging herself. Now she is thanking us, wishing us well, turning, moving back to the jeep and the heels of her sandals smack against her feet as she quickly walks away. Salim bids us farewell and follows her, clenching and unclenching his hand around the car key. The engine coughs itself awake and they drive off down the road and around the two bends, the dust rising up behind them.

Later, after we store the sifted soil and rearrange the half-dried pots in the sun, after tea and after Miriam starts talking again, Khadija pulls the card from her pocket. She reads it silently, and then laughs aloud. Passes it on to Miriam, smiling. By the time it reaches me, Khadija is rattling off plans for our future; this could be a good business for us, a new opportunity. The other two will soon be back from visiting their family in Foro Baranga, and Talah can take on more of the pottery. We have enough hands between us to make this work. And they do have money, these NGOs.

I turn over the card and see Fahima's full name written in shaky script across the top. Beneath it, a foreign name is printed in English – Ron Rivera, PFP. Underneath the initials she has written out a careful translation in Arabic. Potters For Peace.

The goats run up and over the lip of the wadi bank and chase each other through the graveyard of broken pots. The smallest one trails behind, chewing a fragment of dirty white plastic as it runs. When it sees me looking it stumbles to a halt, its mouth clamped possessively around the piece of bag. A smile spreads through me as Khadija laughs and claps her hands together. The goat starts, drops the plastic at its feet, and is gone.

Locusts

ON NIGHTS LIKE THESE the air makes no concession. It just drops, sudden and smothering, no relief till 4am. We sit out against the wall by the road, you beside me in the dark, holding your drink, rolling the glass between two flat palms. We don't speak. Just sit together in silence, knees touching. Listen the neighbours in the next compound, a stream of Arabic over the wall. Shouting. An argument. Maybe an enthusiastic chat. Hard to tell. Not that either of us understands. You swirl the hooch in your glass and over the wall the shouting stops. Spluttering – a woman, I think – like water's gone down the wrong way. Someone spits and then a man speaks, something short and sharp. It's completely silent for a moment, with them, with us, until a sudden wave of sound rolls in from above, static between the stations. A blanket of tiny rustling noises.

Locusts.

We lean back and watch. They ripple and surge ten feet above us, hundreds of thousands of them, maybe millions, a fluttering ceiling of copper-dusted sequins, papery lanterns with no light inside. You tell me that their migration will take weeks. They'll fly over us in a night and only rest when they find water. You press your leg against mine until they pass, half an hour, and then you hold the glass up to my lips till I drain the last mouthful.

You're gone by morning, and no one else is around to care. Paula's on a week long survey of the neighbouring district, and I don't hear J come in until sunrise. When I emerge from my room he's busy in the yard, face inside the generator, tools spread out on the ground behind him.

'Salaam,' I call to him, 'good morning.' One arm goes up and he shouts back in greeting, doesn't turn around. He keeps a low monologue going, talking quietly to the generator and each of its pieces as he works: 'Little piston, what's wrong now, huh, why don't you move, what, you've lost the love little piston?' By the time I've changed my shirt and pants, and washed myself quickly, the generator has growled and coughed and fallen silent twice more. J swears a little more as he sweet talks the pistons and checks each connecting point. He reaches one arm in deep, turns the wrench, and pulls back. Slaps the green start switch and holds the body of the engine as it comes to life. Done. As it settles into a consistent rumble he claps both hands together and lets out a celebratory shout.

'Marcos my brother, how are you?' He bellows over the noise of the generator, grinning wide as I approach 'You have a fun night?' He flips the generator off and then walks over to the kitchen, saying something about coffee and bread and the radio mast that still needs fixing.

Most of our conversations go like this. J speaks, asks a question, then cuts himself off and moves onto something else before it can progress. You sent him over to us after seeing the advertisement. He had a written reference and a personal recommendation: 'Despite having to leave for Nyala at one point due to a family crisis, J arranged his own cover by drafting in a competent and trustworthy trainee, and completed an engine overhaul before he left. Highly motivated, highly skilled, and highly recommended to any organisation working in the area.'

That was a few months ago. Early summer, not hot by Sudanese standards, and you were the only one not sweating in the sun at the back of the security meeting. Paula and I were there shining like beacons, sweat finding ever new paths down our sides and backs, stinking of adrenaline and days spent in the same set of clothes. The Littlest Aid Organisation in the West was how Paula introduced us – just two of us, one truck, one computer. Sat at the back where the French medics passed around cigarettes and spoke in low murmurs through the whole briefing. The chair stood at the front, capping and uncapping his marker pen. He strode back and forth in front of the flipchart and spoke slowly like time was no concern. Good with an audience: exactly who J would have become if he'd been born in Denver instead of a little village on the Chad-Sudan border.

Yours was the only lighter that worked, remember? The medics passed the smokes across the back row and I felt like a kid. Took your lighter. You watched it like a hawk, held your hand out for it once everyone was lit. This isn't a good place for being frivolous, for misplacing things. You slipped it back into your pocket and introduced yourself. Pointed at your name on the WFP letterhead in your lap while the chair read out the list of No-Gos and restricted areas for the week. I wrote my name and organisation on the inside of my palm and showed it to you, like passing a note in school. You held the ends of my fingers while you read it, then swallowed a laugh and nodded, eyes front.

The meeting broke and this time you shook my hand. 'You're working in one of our camps, I think – Ardamata?' I nodded. 'You're the ones looking for a mechanic and technician, right? I might have just the guy. I'll send him over. Come by my office if you need anything else – links with the sheikhs, that kind of thing. We're based right next to the market.' You were the first person to invite us in with something practical. Not that the other agencies hadn't been welcoming, but we're small fry, me and Paula, only able to work in one camp at a time. Around us these huge multinationals build whole settlements, drill for water and feed thousands, and we show up with boxes of exercise books and a football pump. The emergency daycare. Not always easy to get taken seriously, especially when one of you is a guy.

J moved in with us not long after that, and went straight for the room beside the neighbours' compound, the one against the shared wall. Happy to live and work on site, he said it was better for him as his wife and kids lived so far away.

So weird to think of him married, a father. He has the wild eyes of a man from a song, some epic tale delivered in a gravelly voice. I just can't picture him in domesticity, surrounded by family. Maybe he can't either.

J sticks out here. I don't know what it is exactly, but he's always a little too loud, unreserved, and it puts the locals on edge. He walks with his shoulders back and chin up, almost comically so, stroking his small silvering beard to a point. The market stall holders see him coming and flit their eyes, checking to see what's not there – the cash bag? A credit note? He arrives like we arrive: speaking a different language. The traders brace. I see all this cross their faces when we go looking for parts down in the craftsman's end of the market. We pass the carpenter, then the man selling electrical goods. Look away from the white hot arc in the open door of the welding shop. Just round the corner is the part of the market that burned down six months ago, maybe seven. Eaten up by the torches of janjaweed fighters, revenge for resistance. A proud businessman refused to pay the tithe demanded, or maybe it was done just for effect... no one really knows. Seven died that night, others lost all their stock.

'Brother!' J bellows into the open front of the mechanic's shop. The man at the counter flinches a little when J claps his hands together and holds his arms open like he's ready to take a dance partner. 'A gasket is all we need, so make me smile and tell me you've got the one we want, my good Bahar.' Bahar smiles with some effort and leans on the layers of wood and cardboard that form his shop counter, every little strip and off-cut fitted flush to the front. J's voice is theatrical, a matinee idol. Bahar smiles evenly at J, at me, and pulls out a small piece of paper and a short pencil. He speaks slowly. 'So tell me then, brother, about this engine you need to save.'

J swaggers across the shop and I leave them to it, stand out on the street and light a cigarette. They could be a while. Across the road a white guy with an expensive camera faces us, shooting, and I look right down the lens before he turns and walks away.

I'm not far from your office. J's still deep in conversation with Bahar, so I've got time for a walk. I make my way through the throng of buyers and sellers, tired animals and overstocked carts. A man roars about the quality of his snakeskin shoes – the price! Incredible! A bow-backed donkey laden with full water bladders and a chapped hard-on brays at a tree. A tea stand is assembled. Greetings, hands gripped, shoulders slapped, how's the family?

Two teenage boys turn into the street ahead of me, hand in hand, chewing fingernails, eyes everywhere. An easy grace, and it's allowed. Snake hips and long lashes and it's allowed: the kind of male friendships that don't wash back home. I've had fingers broken for less.

I watch the boys as I cross the road to where you stand at your gate. You watch them too, tip your head when you see me. 'You know the penalty is death,' you tell me as I reach your side. 'They can hold hands with their best friend in the world, strut down the street together, arm in arm and totally invisible like Queen Victoria's dykes,' you say, 'because they don't exist. They're an impossibility. Khawaji, totally foreign.'

I can smell you, smell your sweat, or maybe it's mine. I call you later to say thanks for the help, and to hear your voice again. Don't sleep that night.

*

I arrived in Vancouver underweight and broke, fourteen and knowing way too much already about prairie justice and the desperate failings of adults. Fourteen and wound so tight with adrenaline it was weeks before I slowed to a walking pace. Running. Hiding. Scaling tall buildings with a single bound, I was invincible then. Broke out, then broke in. Ended up in a shelter on the edge of Low Track. Three years I stayed there as a resident, off and on. By the time I got my high school diploma I was working nights on the front desk a few times a week. Turns out I'm a good listener.

When the building got condemned and the funding pulled we all moved on to different centres. I was management by then. Well, that was the title. Ended up helping out at a few other places till eventually I was running a long-stay project just outside the city centre, then that got pulled too.

I still needed to feed myself, needed to get paid to do something, right? A small ad in an email bulletin: please forward attached to your contacts. Initial contract for six months, field post, salary subject to negotiation. No strings, ready to go. Set up a pilot centre in one major camp for Internally Displaced Peoples in West Darfur, providing support to unaccompanied minors – programme delivery and referral. Links to educational and healthcare services as appropriate. Primarily setting up and delivering a programme of therapeutic support and mentoring, with the aim of community integration. Children who've seen things no one should see. The unrepeatable.

Even after more than a decade of working with kids who've endured the worst kinds of abuse, of addiction and neglect, I have no precedent for this, for the sheer scale of it.

There's a boy in the camp centre, ten, missing half his skin. Scar tissue all down his chest and legs. Dragged behind a horse. He's so damaged inside that he cries every time he needs to shit, his body a maze of wrong turns.

There's a girl, seven, no teeth, punched out, smashed out on the day she lost her whole family. More stories than there will ever be words to tell.

We get them drawing pictures instead of talking. This one is a school, a favourite playing place, the flat piece of land beside the wadi. Here's where the football got stuck in the tree, so high it took a whole day to retrieve, all the boys together, and then Mohammed broke his foot bone when he jumped down. Here's a favourite doll made from bright pieces of tobe and a peg. 'See? She's dressed the same as I was, like mango flesh.' There are other shades of orange in the pictures. Tangerine rips through pages and pages, crimson splashing and pooling in the corners, collecting beneath horizontal figures. We order more coloured pencils. We scan and send the drawings to our head office, far away.

There are often hiding spots in these pictures. Bushes, riverbanks, bodies. One girl draws her donkey running with a thatch of lit grass strapped to its back, burning and burning and running through the compound to the main hut where it will collapse and take everything with it. In another, a woman in her tobe, a baby, all wrapped in flame. The men in green loom large in these pictures. Their helicopters, their guns drawn in detail. Kalashnikov, Antonov, the two Russian words that everyone knows. 'These men here, they are forcing the woman and girl to be wife.'

We play cooperation games with them. Sometimes there's progress, a big leap. Sudden eye contact or the start of a long stream of words. Usually it moves slower. Aliyyah, a teacher and an IDP herself, runs most of the sessions. She plays mother hen to many of the kids, rounding them up, the firm hand full of care. Two other women assist her. I'm the only one here who doesn't really speak Arabic. I can relate to the children through translation, or with shrugs, rolling eyes, and big arm gestures. You laugh when I tell you this. I stick to what I know – logistics, the paperwork. Boring and necessary. You see me gesturing cartoon-like to the children the day you come by the community hut to check on us, and call me Punch from then on. I act annoyed. It doesn't deter you.

'I know all the words to the diarrhoea song,' I say, as Aliyyah starts it up with the group, clapping time.

We wash our hands/we wash our hands/with soap and water/with soap and water/to stop the diarrhoea/to stop the diarrhoea/we stay strong/we stay strong.

This is as poetic as my Arabic gets. We clean our hands. Then we bring out the tubs of bread and fruit, we sit with the kids and we eat.

Fourteen was bad. It was a bad year. Sleeping in car parks, finding beds any way I could, eventually the shelter. Cold, a lot of the time. Before that, thirteen. Holes in walls. Holes the size of fists, the size of heads. Blood thicker than water, thick as a scab that keeps getting torn, I am your family, boy, and you do as I say. A one-man terror squad, he was. Attacks in the night, guerrilla style, stealing each of my things one by one till I had just the clothes I lay in. Stripped, hearing her on the other side of the bedroom wall, hearing her through the holes as she tried not to make a sound. Purple in the morning, a scary smile that didn't bend right. Twelve. She was still intact when I was twelve. She knew. Knew about me and told me she loved me anyhow, that no matter what, love was the one thing worth anything, son, worth everything to her. He was there then, prowling round the edges, watching, controlling my time with her. That last year with her was the worst. The best and the worst – her opening right out like a rose bloom before it really dies, that intoxicating smell, the colours so deep. I saw all of it then, felt all of it. In those moments before it ended, I knew what came next so I breathed it in and tried to hold every lungful as long as I could, tried to make that smell a part of me, take it with me when I left for good.

You're sat beside me in the yard when I tell you this, turning your lighter over and over. You're quiet. Fuck. Now I'm talking way too much, spilling out my whole sad story. 'Tell me a secret,' I say. 'Or a joke with an amazing punch line, anything.' It's now midnight, way past curfew. If you get back in your truck now you're taking your chances, risky roads at this time of night. As if for confirmation, a gun cracks out two shots from the direction of the market. An answer shot replies. And another.

'Here's something amazing,' you say, and you lean in, and you tell me.

★

J's been drinking. He drank before, but he's really been drinking since Paula's been away. Didn't want to let loose in front of the lady, perhaps. He smells of fermented dates and each morning is quieter than before. Wound tight. Never quite drunk at work, but getting close.

'I can't sleep in that room,' he tells me when I ask why he's been sleeping on a mat outside the kitchen. 'I need to get away from the neighbours' wall. I need the sky above me, some air,' he says. His beard is growing in patches across his cheeks and chin. The silvery point is starting to matt. He works as hard as ever, now weatherproofing all the electrics for the rainy season. 'Still a few months away, but we must be ready,' he tells me.

The sleeping mat moves, right up to the front gate where the truck is parked – the furthest point from the neighbour's wall. I offer him my room as a swap. 'You can't sleep outside in the rain, J, you need some shelter.' He won't do it. He clears his few belongings to one side of his old room and just uses it as storage. Spends no more than a few minutes in there each day, and always during daylight.

On one particularly insomniac night, I decide to move myself into his abandoned room. Perhaps he'll take mine if I'm out of it already, if the shifting has already been done. Once I've carried over my few possessions, I make the bed, light a candle and lay back, waiting for daybreak.

'Marcos.' I'm returning from the kitchen with a coffee when he stops me.

'Morning J, how'd you sleep?' I ask. His hands are on his hips as he speaks.

'This room by the neighbour's wall is not good for you. You must move back.' His eyes crackle like coals on a low fire.

'It's fine,' I tell him. 'No problem. You stay in my old room, I stay in this one.' His face is deadpan. 'You can't sleep in the rain J, so just move your stuff into the empty room and we'll both be fine.' No response. I've never seen him like this. A muscle in his jaw flickers and he doesn't blink. Just turns around and walks away.

That night I lie in J's abandoned room and drift between sleep and wake, images and sounds fanning through me. Ten years old; rodeo fairground, ice cream, one eye closed against the sun, the other on all the girls, all the boys. Fourteen; screaming, not me, screaming, dark room but the moon is half full. Fifteen; screaming, me full of joy on a roller coaster, throwing up afterwards, don't care. First blowjob. First hand held. In love and I feel sick. Nineteen; funeral, moon half full. Can't cry. Want to. Can't. He's there and I don't cry. Twenty; phone call from neighbour to tell me he's dead. Buy myself the hugest bunch of red flowers and put them in my room. Don't care if it looks faggy, they smell amazing. I'm alive and the flowers smell amazing. Twenty eight; on the bed facing the thin wall, the neighbour's wall, and it's still dark. Door open. The smell from outside fills the room, hangs over me, sweet and thick, that trail of pink that runs along the window frame, pink that looks like leaves, grows in a vine, next to small white swirly stars. Screaming. The moon is half full. Crack, something hits the wall. Crack. Pink flowers, and white. Frangipani. That smell. Crack. Scream. Breathe in, breathe out. I must have left the mozzie net off and now the ants are walking on my face, whispering feet, loud breathing, 'Marcos.' Heavy breathing. 'Marcos. I have to go man. I'm going.' J's face is inches from mine when I open my eyes. His breath is like old pennies. His face is wet. 'I'm leaving. I'll come back if I can, but for now I go.' J is panting. His teeth show. He is panting when he leaves, when I stand, when I make it to the door to see him closing the gate and disappearing into the night.

The far wall of J's bedroom isn't a proper wall. The whole room was just built right up against the compound edge, the outer wall shared with the neighbours. A sound like a siren is coming from the other side. Like a broken siren that clicks on and off, again and again. She is crying. I hear her through the breeze blocks and mud, like a faulty alarm. I go back to my bed and I lie down again, feel ashamed for doing so, fucking coward, but lie still, barely moving to breathe. When the first light hits the sky she is at the gate, banging. I let her in. Fatima, I think. I say, 'Salaamu'alikum, sabah el kheir,' like an idiot tourist and she lets her scarf fall back across messy hair. The side of her face is swollen, her skin shines.

'Mister,' she says. 'Where is he? Where is Jamil?'

I stumble over an answer that's no good to her at all. 'I…I don't know.'

'Good,' she says, before I can get another word out. Good. She studies each of my eyes in turn, then leaves.

I don't mention this brief visit when the police question me later that day. I just don't. The translation process makes it easy to leave it out. Her husband was found dead in his room in the early hours of the morning. Fatima got up to light the stove, looked round the open door, and there he was on his bed, head caved in, smashed beyond recognition. Terrible.

'Terrible,' they say in the market. 'So terrible to meet this end. And now J is gone, that madman, disappeared. Always a strange man, a bad man.' 'I never trusted him.' 'No, no neither did I' – they talk and they talk. I'm just a stupid khawaji, know nothing worth knowing, so I am exonerated, and everyone is so so sorry.

In my head I invent explanations, convince myself of one thing then unpick it with another. Maybe he was a gambling man, J. A man of many debts. Risk taker. Big talker. Pulled one over on the wrong man, took the wrong guy for a ride so had to cut his losses and move on. Or he was a drinker. Bottles of home brew, methanol tinged, known to bring out the beast in the calmest of men. Paranoia. Delusion. Or he was a seducer. A ladies man who took what he wanted then faced the wrath of the husband he'd shamed. Or maybe he was a vigilante fighter, hearing things through the wall. Hearing his neighbour in distress, beaten by her husband on the other side of the breeze blocks and mud, night after night. Maybe he could no longer stand to hear it, not another slap, not a single punch more.

What if one night he hears, and he goes next door. He confronts the man, face to face, looks him right in the eye and calls him the coward and low life shit that he is. They fight. The man swings at him, outraged at having his authority challenged, in his own home no less, and J ducks. He grabs the man unawares and hits him. He hits him and he hits him with something hard, a torque wrench, till the man lies still. What if he is brave enough to do all that?

You leave your office as soon as you hear, drive fast, arrive wide eyed with your hands jumping up and down to cover your mouth. 'Thank god you're ok,' you say. 'I'm so sorry. Who could have known he was such a fucking psycho?' I think of telling you right then about my vigilante theory, that he might have done the very best he could do, stood up rather than walked away, that J might be a hero, but I don't. I swallow. You take out your lighter with a shaky hand, light your cigarette. The glow of the flame catches on wings and shells as around us lie the bodies of the locusts that didn't make it, the ones that hit the wall as they flew over us that night, looking for water and rest somewhere a long way from here.

The Rig

SHE'D BEEN WAITING IN Zalingei for five days now: phone calls back to Alex in the Mornei office, and Simon at her side reassuring her that the permit was sorted, properly stamped this time, and it was on its way, definitely, no question. Simon was her number two, at least until they had the water system up and running in the new camp, and so when he stood in the office doorway with his face set in grim apology, she dug her nails into the desk and readied herself for more bad news.

'I need to show you something,' he said. 'You'd better see for yourself.' He led her out onto the street and turned back to her, his arms thrown wide.

'Ta da!' he exclaimed, as the driver sounded the horn. Here it was, blocking the road; a huge blue truck with the drilling rig crouched across its back like a praying mantis of nightmare proportions. Twelve tonnes of potential. Quite beautiful.

After they manoeuvred it into the yard, Gloria spent more than an hour checking it over. It wasn't as high spec as some of the newer rigs she'd seen. This was more of a workhorse, but it would do everything they needed, and besides, she preferred the manual dials. She ran her finger around the faces of the compression and torque gauges, and wiped a smudge from the glass. Only one other organisation had a rotary rig this far west, and that one was currently working the camps that clustered around Geneina. Gloria's rig was destined for the wild, dry lands that lay north of Zalingei town and the green slopes of Jebel Marra. When they first visited Kurni, back in March, it was a small village, one of many that dotted the banks of the Wadi Nang'illey. It hosted only a handful of escapees: a few families who'd fled the violence that was swallowing the neighbouring villages whole. Now Kurni was becoming a camp, five hundred new arrivals and more every day, with just one well between them. Two people had died already, digging into the wadi bed in search of the murky water below, using spades, buckets, hands. Three metres down before collapsing walls of wet sand buried them. The most desperate of deaths.

The attacks on the villages were now near-constant, which meant a growing mass of homeless people. Most went to the big camps – Abata, and the one on the edge of Zalingei – but others found refuge with neighbours in places like Kurni. With the findings from the March survey and the results from the test pumping last month, Gloria now had two confirmed sites for boreholes and a network of tap stands that could supply everyone in growing Kurni for the foreseeable future. Simon had assembled the rest of the drilling team, and Gloria had finished the designs. The final piece was the rig, and, at last, it was here. They were ready to break ground.

That night, Simon organised a barbecue in celebration. A sheep was killed and the rig anointed with its blood: Gloria's handprint in red, fingers spread across the end of the main mast. The cook gathered the cleaning girls and the three of them sang a tribute in their mother tongue, then another in Arabic. Neighbours arrived from nearby agencies to wish them well and share the food, and Gloria found herself happy to stay with the group, letting the glow of the gathering hold her. They raised the mast and locked it vertical and as the sun sank, Gloria climbed onto the control platform and turned the key. The assembled crowd cheered as the engine roared to life and the drill shaft spun. A warm wind rolled in, making slow dancers of a napkin and a paper plate and by the time curfew came at nine the guests were gone, the kitchen side of the compound littered with little bits of paper.

Since her arrival, she had seen two coordinators come and go, both redeployed to Ache after the tsunami. Alex was the third, dividing his time between here and the office in Mornei. Simon, their logs guy, was the only constant. They were right at the centre of the continent, with nomadic lands stretching for hundreds of miles on all sides – across Chad to the west, and the vast lands of the Darfurs to the north, south and east.

'The Siberia of Africa' was how the Georgian medic described their temporary home. Marta had been sent in after sickness had swept through both offices several times in the last few months. She was an ex-midwife and nurse, and she talked and she talked and amidst the frantic pace of work, the daily struggle to get another water system operating in another quadrant of another camp, Marta wanted intimate details. Friendly chats about mental health and bowel movements. She wanted to shine torches down everyone's throats.

It was during dinner one night that Marta asked, 'Are you married, Gloria?'

'No,' she replied. She could have said more, could have mentioned the family home in the Ngong Hills, her young son Leon, her sister and their mother, the unusual arrangement, but instead she watched as the cat crept up on a beetle, teasing it with one paw.

'If you stay out here another six months you'll be as strong as the mast on that rig,' Simon said. 'You can work pretty much anywhere then.' This led into the usual conversation of where and how long and how hard everyone's previous assignments had been and all the while that beetle ran and ran in the same eight inch circle in the sand, every potential escape route blocked by a quick white paw. By the time the cat tired of the game, Marta had gone to bed.

Gloria sat in silence with Simon and her mind soon turned to the rig. It was from India, built to order for the desert. It wasn't the exact one she would have liked, but pretty damn good considering how hard it was to get anything at all shipped out here. It had a five metre mast and a hefty air compressor, perfect for difficult sites like the camp. She'd been assured several times over that the hydraulics would withstand the fine sand that found its way in between every moving part. Last week she bought a Toyota pickup from one of the other agencies, and it was now loaded with casing for the boreholes. After all the planning, she wanted to get out there, start drilling.

'So what about family?' Simon spoke in a soft voice now, just loud enough for one set of ears. 'Do you think you'll have kids, get married?' Family. The ones back home. She could tell the truth – about her son, her sister, her brother-in-law. About the negotiation that had gone into that particular arrangement, the dovetail of her own needs with her sister's. Is that what he wanted to know? That she was an absent parent like him, like every father out here, sending home rent and the fees for Leon's Nairobi school. That she had handed the child over willingly and still woke each night feeling him heavy in the cavities of her body. 'You should have been a man,' Mum had said once, not unkindly. With time, and the money she was able to send back, it became mostly accepted by the few who knew.

Last time she phoned home they had a decent line and time to speak. Leon had just finished the term at school and was back home, ready for a summer of long playful days in the hills. Mum had picked him up, and as they drove past the airport Leon pointed and told his school friend, 'That's where auntie lives.' He was half right, Gloria thought, and it didn't upset her to hear it.

Out here, she had to make a stand-in family; the skinny white cat and its chicken bone ribs, the water donkeys that arrived at the gate each morning and the bug-eyed boys who beat them with strips of rawhide. She could have made friends with anyone: the shadows, and the wide stretches of sand and grit that wound past the truck windows as they drove out to the drill sites. Once in a while she felt the old bones of home in all this unfamiliar land, just occasionally, and she had no way of saying this without getting it wrong, being mistaken for someone who was running. It was the same on all these jobs. Liberia, Ingushetia, DRC. Home was in the moving, eyes on the horizon.

'If marriage is what you want, this work will ruin you,' Simon told her when she didn't answer him. He let the silence close in for a moment. 'Sorry.' He said it like she should be crushed, or at least a little insulted. If she was offended, she didn't show it. She let a faint smile light her face, and she swallowed the last drop of water from her cup.

They set off at dawn, and as noon approached they were well past the halfway point despite the slow pace of their convoy. Gloria rode in the lead vehicle in front of the rig, with Marta and Simon following behind in the pickup. The road narrowed after Gudai and took them through a deep wadi bed, a slow struggle for the rig. Twenty miles more till they'd hit Kurni. On the other side of the wadi, the track turned down and to the left, and as they rounded the corner, there before them was a military-style truck with canvas-covered back. It was converted to civilian use with white and blue paint on each side and a rough insignia on the doors. It was slumped at the side of the road. They pulled in and stopped, approached on foot. Three of the tyres were flat. Small ragged holes cut through the metal of the doors, and the sand beneath the tank was ridged where petrol had spilled and dried. The back of the truck hung open. It was empty but for a single green bucket, new and shiny and cracked down one side. A delivery for the camp.

There had been no word of this on the radio. They walked to the brow of the hill to see what was ahead and there, in a shallow ditch, lay a body dressed in white. He was shoeless, the soles of his feet badly swollen and caked with dark sand. His arms lay high above his head, reaching for the road. Marta kneeled beside him, moved one of his arms, checked his pulse, listened for the breath that wasn't there and before she looked up again she smoothed a wrinkle from his jellabiya.

His ID was still around his neck, the laminate card caught beneath his head. A delivery driver for one of the agencies. Salim. Small features, with a neat moustache. Gloria called it in, first to her own base and then to AU and UN security. She clipped the handset back onto her belt and poured a little water onto her palms, held them over her face. They were told to wait here for the soldiers. The nearest AU base was 45 minutes away on clear roads and this fell within their mandate: monitoring, non-engagement. They would come and ask questions of Gloria and Marta and Simon and then they would collect the body and return it to the hospital in Zalingei. There it would lie in the morgue and its family would come, *his* family would come, and the AU would inform OCHA who would inform countless other agencies that there had been another killing of humanitarian personnel.

Gloria shook the water from her hands and wondered who had ordered this. Which of the 51 most wanted? There were many more than 51 individuals who carried out butchery, of course, but the list of key players was an open secret: guessed at by many and seen by few, the war criminals. As well as the obvious candidates, the military men – the Musa Hilals and Hamid Dawais, captains of the death squads – there were others, the desk killers, the bureaucrats who sat in Khartoum offices and directed the war by mobile phone. She met one of these men once, during her first week in Sudan, she was sure of it. A Minister for West Darfur. They met at the Embassy Club, one in a crowd of big men she was introduced to; he stood out, moving slow and deliberate. She didn't make the connection until seeing his name in a briefing document months later. He was no warlord, not like Hilal. This one hadn't worked his way through the ranks, a career soldier with a flair for strategy and the kind of forceful nature that brings men in line. This man's office was up on the hill, near the Sultan's house in Geneina. He had soft hands and still eyes. Knew Swahili, charmed everyone he met. He didn't speak loudly. Didn't have to.

On the roadside, Marta sat at the head of the dead man and waved the flies away from his face. 'Don't you need to leave them so they can establish time of death from the eggs?' Gloria said, immediately appalled by her words. Marta didn't look up.

It was much later, when the night was at its deepest and the convoy was parked in a circular formation at the edge of the village, that Gloria went alone to the rig. It was on the camp side, their field tents pitched behind. The drill shaft had been locked vertical, ready for the morning. They would check the jacks and secure the wing bit, cut down through the topsoil, and then, once they'd changed to the rotor bit, it would be rock. She would stand at the back so she could monitor the progress, cuttings spraying out from the diverter, six hours in the sun, at least. She pressed her fingers against the base and traced the truck's length as she walked round it, one side to the other, until she stood directly below the handprint at the top of the drill shaft, still visible. The metal was radiating the last of the day's heat. She held the side of her face against the rig and looked up to the bloody palm above. The wind changed direction. A phone rang.

Marta appeared, holding the satphone. 'It's your sister,' she said, and a host of possibilities rushed in, all of them featuring Leon's face, all subtitled with panic. Gloria took the phone and Marta retreated.

'Glory.' Her sister sounded small. 'It's happened again. She's in the hospital now, I'm with her and – she's been out for 24 hours. Mum had another stroke.'

Mum. This one made three. Three that they knew of. Her sister talked quickly: when, where, room of the house, time of day, that chair with the loose arm and Gloria's mind ran. Another. The first time they didn't even know about it. Happened in the night, invisible like a dream that left well before morning. Only discovered when stroke number two occurred. Number Two was large, dramatic. A broken glass coffee table and Leon screaming. Leon screaming and the birds erupting from the tree by the window. The recovery was slow. Gloria was there for some of it.

Now her sister's voice spoke like the doctors had. 'We knew it was only a matter of time. This might not have even been the third. There may have been others.' She sounded tired. 'I have to go,' she said, 'but I'll call again tomorrow. I'll keep you up to date if anything changes.' She cried into the phone, and then offered a quick goodbye before the call swallowed the last of her phone card.

Number three.

Gloria sank against the wheel of the truck, ready to wait the night out beneath the rig. She closed her eyes and there it was – her mother's face, luminous against the deep green of the garden, the smell of her childhood home rising like steam between them as the river ran splashing and leaping past the house. She would visit Leon soon, she decided; take him on holiday, to the coast perhaps, and by the time she had made the list of what and where and how, the first streams of light were breaking over the horizon in thin waves.

A plastic bag hopped out from under the truck and danced before her, spinning as the wind picked up. The canvas of the field tents cracked and slapped and the air began to take on some kind of solid form, heavy like rocks. The sky was moving. The plastic bag turned and turned, flung itself, circling up until the wind snatched it away. The desert suddenly leapt into the air and a fury of sand came at her from all sides. Her eyes snapped shut. She pulled her scarf over her face and through interlocked lashes all she saw was red, flying in every direction, pushing back the rising sun: a dust storm.

Over the scream of the wind the rig tolled above her as the drill mast fought against the lock and brace that held it vertical. She reached down for something solid, something to grip. A stone came loose in one hand. Sand in the other. She dug down again, again, harder, further down this time, and again, until she was wrist deep in the ground, digging, sand below and above and on every side. She braced herself against the wheel well, pushing back with both heels, and pumped her arms, clawed the ground. Nails bending, fingers curled tight and insistent. The further she dug the cooler the sand, cool and still, stillness, somewhere down there. As she dug, the rig shook. It shook in the wind, the sound of the mast hitting its brace and counting for her — dig, dig, dig. It was a hollow sound, not a bell or a gong, more hammer on anvil, a noise that travelled through bone, a dull thud that came with each breath and dug for her. She let her hands hang still as the rig bit down, eating through sand, through soil, that first vein of rock and then bedrock, through the bedrock. She felt herself fall the whole length of it, fingers scraping the walls and marking the faintest of routes on the way down and, despite the depth there at the bottom, she still heard it; she heard the rig as it thrashed through the storm above her, a mournful voice singing out into the dark of the new day.

About the Farmhouse

SEVENTEEN WEEKS IN. The food is terrible but I don't eat much anyway, so it doesn't matter. I used to say that my taste buds died the day I signed up; crew cut, uniform, willingness to eat shit. Not much has changed in that respect, but at least here we make our own dinner at night – the only time I'm hungry.

I'm the chip cook. Anna peels potatoes with me, Joseph does the meat. Alan does nothing because he's a lazy cunt and Mirko cooks like a man who married young, so he washes the dishes. Once a week Joseph makes a curry so hot that we have to coordinate it with whatever beer is available.

When we were a team of ugly men we were ignored, but since Anna arrived five weeks ago we get regular invites to the UN parties, and so weekly access to their pipeline. We've also got a hook-up through one of the AU soldiers – apparently Joseph went to school with him in Kampala. He brings bottles of whiskey from across the Chad border. 'Cameroonian Finest Blend' it says on the label. Rough as fuck, but better than the janjaweed juice, and good for when the beer dries up.

This week we're hiring a programme assistant, so today we spend all morning and most of the afternoon interviewing. I tried to get out of it, told Anna to just make her decision and let me know, but she wouldn't have it. Said it was a team decision, so she made me sit through seven hours.

Late afternoon we break for the day, and Alan calls me over to the radio room. A message just came through. He tells me that our supply truck has been hit on the way to the Kurni Camp drop off. It happened just past Gudai, called in by a convoy heading out there with a drilling rig. Salim, our driver, is dead. They found his body in the ditch.

★

'ON YOUR FEET SOLDIER!'

I'm out of bed before my eyes have time to focus. The air in the tent is stale and hot, armpits, farts and bad breath and something sharp digs into my heel as I stand straight.

Someone's laughing. Stefan.

'Stupid cunt,' I groan, falling back into my bed. He slaps the soles of my feet.

'I've got an officer's voice, haven't I? A nice timbre. Maybe even Colonel, you think?' He clears his throat loudly and bellows again, this time even lower.

'Oooooooonnn yoooooooooouuuuuurrr…'

'Fuck off Stefan.'

He won't stop now that he's on a roll. He keeps shouting as I come to – 'This is a direct order Sergeant, hands off your cock, chin up, shoulders back, and what the fuck is that all over your face? Ever heard of a razor you slovenly shit?' – on and on till I give in and sit up.

'Enough!' I shout. 'I'm up.'

Today we're both off on leave. One week. We take the train to Belgrade and tonight we go down to the Sava.

We meet Mila and Sofia at the station then go home to ditch our bags and wash. We take them to Gypsy Island for dinner on the river, their choice. Mila's favourite place in the city. Nice food, coffee, wine. The first few days of seeing her again, the first night especially, I feel sick with relief at being with her, and nervous like a boy on his first date, twitching around conversation. Horny. I'd go anywhere she wanted, I don't care. By eleven or twelve we're back across the river and moving from club to club, Mila and Sofia showing us all the new places, and they're dancing with their arms flung wide, swinging each other around and then pulling us in close. Even I'm dancing. We do shots at this place that's blaring Ceca, one after the next, and Sofia shouts, 'I hate this! Let's go, there's better music at Crush,' so we move on to a huge boat with a gleaming black floor that looks deep like the river at night. Two women in long skirts and a shirtless man dance on tables near the door, cracking their heels against the wood, and the crowd cheers as the tempo picks up. We step onto the deck and I'm hit full in the chest with a blast of trumpets. Mila turns and smiles as a new beat kicks in. The boat rocks, the floor shakes.

*

Today I should be resting. If I'd stayed at home with a shitty job that paid not quite enough to move my family to an apartment with two bedrooms, I could have spent today walking down to the river to watch the geese pick through the leftovers of Saturday night.

I could go to church and sing alongside the rest of my street. I could try to stretch out the day. Moan about tomorrow's work, worry about money.

I could have sex with my wife. Fall asleep on the sofa so she can have space in our single bed. I could wake at 4 a.m. with a stiff neck, turn over, drift, and get up two hours later. I could roam. Find myself bored and wanting. No other woman, no other family, but wanting.

Instead I am here, in yet another desert, counting bags full of greasy dinars and filling our bank account with thin paper promises.

Here in Darfur, I wake at 4 a.m. with a stiff neck. I lie on a hard-framed bed, metal slats digging through an inch of foam as I count gunshots in the dark. I get up at six, tie sand-coloured boots, tuck sand-coloured trousers over their tops. I eat less, fast more, mention it to no one and watch my skin grow sand coloured too in the shard of mirror in my room.

Out here, I wear a t-shirt. Sometimes a canvas vest at night after the sun has dropped, but nothing heavy. No armour or equipment storage packs. I'm living light, the way I wanted to for years. The others complain about the hardship of this place – the heat, the food, the bullets – but all I feel is light.

★

'We'll go camping,' I tell him, 'next time.' Miloš is sulking. He's upset that I'm leaving again. I tell him I'll miss him. He'll get used to it. It's better for him, for us all, to have me working away. He looks up at me with big puppy eyes.

'Go to school,' I say. 'Take care of your mother. Protect her.' She's been protecting herself for most of her life but it makes us both feel better to talk about her like this, like it's her who needs us. He gives me a stern nod.

She comes in and places her hands on his shoulders. Tells him to get his shoes.

She looks me in the eye. 'Mila…' I say, and now her head is just below mine, her hair touching my nose. Her arms are on my waist and her smell is inside me. I breathe deep, a whole lung full. We stand like this, breathing in and out together, until Miloš appears at the doorway, clomping in his school shoes.

'Let's go little man,' she says, and kisses me once on the mouth before taking Miloš by the hand and leading him out the door.

I stand in the stairwell and watch as their heads spiral slowly down, floor by floor. They reach the bottom and look up.

'Wave bye bye,' she tells him, and he does.

★

The interviews are over and I have my man: Mohammed. Tall and quiet, fastidious. He doesn't flinch like the others when I speak. When I tell him he has a week to ask me as many questions as he wants, then no more, he understands and starts right away, writing notes in a small book.

It might just be the new job enthusiasm that has him alert and working now, a temporary state before he backslides into the little-as-possible crawl. We'll see. If he does turn out to be a lazy ass who makes fatur last an hour and a half, he won't have time to get a charming smile out onto his face.

'I'm not babysitting,' I tell Anna. She lifts her eyebrows and says nothing, just spreads the payroll papers across the tables in the centre of our office, along with the hundreds of notes that we'll deliver to the field offices in a gym bag. A three day round trip.

Anna is counting out the salaries. She gets a different number each time she counts the main stack in front of her, again and again. She starts swearing, going red in the face.

'It's only paper,' I tell her. 'Count it again. Don't get upset.' She begins again. 'You know, the best finance staff come from countries where the currency has collapsed. No real attachment to it, to the paper,' I say. No light in the eyes at the big figures. Anna's face is still flushed. She doesn't look up, so I sit and help her to count out another gym bag of money, flicking through tattered bills till both our hands are stained with dirt.

No sleep at all that night. Instead of drifting off for a few hours early morning I sit in the chair outside my room all through the night, feeling the sweat evaporate, listening to the grasshoppers head-butting the wall. Smoking and smoking.

I am inside finding my vest when the night splits with two loud cracks above my head. Screams. I move quickly, find Anna wide-eyed outside on the steps of her room, shaking. I run to the gate, to the street, and see two small figures disappear round the corner. Kids. Our tin roofs make bricks sound like small bombs in the middle of the night.

I sit up till Anna goes back to her room, then I pace till dawn, ready for the fight that doesn't come.

★

The air is full of smoke and cordite that rises with each pop. Bullets pierce through Belgrade's sky, becoming real only when they hit something on the way up – a window, a building – or fall back down to earth and anyone that might be standing on it.

'Get away from the windows.' Miloš is excited. He has just had his first beer, half a beer, while we watched the game together. The Black and Whites have finally won after two ties; the city is wild with joy and vodka.

'Miloš. Away.' He moves back to the chair he just leapt from.

Now we wait inside for the shooting to ease off.

'The bullets fly when we lose, and when we *win…*' Stefan's eyes always used to bulge at that point for comic emphasis. He'd taken one of those footy bullets in the arm once, just a graze. He'd push his sleeve up when the final scores were in, once he was drunk, and make the two torn sides of the scar talk the post-match analysis.

His boy will be nine now. Ten. Too young to remember much of his father.

We pick the boy up each Sunday and bring him to church. I tell him about his father sometimes – funny things, like the scar, and his awful singing voice. I try to help him remember someone he never really knew.

His mother comes too. Sofia. Doesn't say much. Half-smiles, watches me with a heavy eye.

We slept together once, after Stefan died. I suppose her grief was matched by mine. That seemed as good a reason as any to end up in bed together.

'He died in service to his country,' the letter said, and I could have laughed if it'd just been me and Stefan. He could have read it out to me with his scar, flapping the sides of its mouth, wrapping the severed edges around official words that had been spat onto paper without ever being spoken out loud.

But that's not how it was. We were alone together that day, Sofia and me, so I kept my mouth shut and jumped into a hole with her instead. It never happened again. Just once. That desire evaporated quickly, if desire was ever its right name.

★

Today is Thursday. Tomorrow our day off.

By about 9.30 we've drunk enough to forget this place and pretend that we're all old friends, just hanging out. Joseph has an old-fashioned guitar that he borrowed from the translator. He's been trying to tune it for the last half an hour, but the head's bent back at an angle. The thing looks like a lute. Alan is talking about war, about politics and the past and I don't join in.

'Joseph! You're torturing that guitar!' I shout.

Alan throws his arms around as he talks, one of those impassioned Americans who wants to save the world.

'So you think the best policy is non-engagement?' he says. 'Just stand back and let it happen while we keep patching up the wounds as best as we can?'

'No,' says Mirko. 'That's not what I said. My point is that if the AU mandate changes to active engagement, we'll just have another armed group in the mix. That's all. There's not enough of them to stop the attacks, so there's more potential for it to get messy if they can return or open fire, more civilian casualties. Can't you see that?'

He's getting annoyed.

'You're misunderstanding me,' Alan says. 'I'm just questioning the monitoring mandate. It's useless in terms of protection, it implies permission...'

I can smell the rot of a dead animal coming from nearby. I wonder about burning it. The flies are gone from the air now, replaced by grasshoppers and moths and flying worms. The bats spin and dive inches above our heads, gorging on the night time treats attracted by the cold light of our solar lamps.

'...and it's happened again and again. You know that, of all people. Srebrenica, for example – ' Alan won't leave it alone.

'What?'

'Srebrenica,' Alan goes on. 'If there had been more – '

BOOM. Mirko explodes.

'Srebrenica! You think that was the only place where bad things happened? Fucking hell!' He chops the air with his hands. Alan doesn't speak. No one else speaks.

'My village was also bombed, also set on fire. And what about Krajina? Ever heard of that? No? They didn't tell you about that on Fox News, did they, you fucking idiot. Don't fucking talk to me about more guns.'

The last string on Joseph's guitar is loose. It keeps slipping. I want to take it from him and tighten it myself, restring it. I'm sure it's not strung right.

'Joseph, that string...' He nods, stretches his mouth into something that is not a smile. 'My friend, you do a good job.'

I raise my glass to him, to his strange old guitar with the string that won't sing. We need music. I shut my eyes and for a second I can't hear anything. I hold my glass up to my face and the whiskey fills my nose, covers the smell of the donkey rotting on the other side of the compound wall.

★

The last time I saw Sofia was on one of the Sunday visits in Belgrade; I can see us all, walking on the beach on Big War Island, Mila and the kids ahead. Sofia walks beside me for a long time not saying anything. She smokes her cigarette down to the filter, flicks it onto the ground.

'He told me,' she says at last. She lets it hang in the air. 'About the farmhouse.'

The season is turning, a cold wind whipping the surface of the water into little silver waves that rush away from the bank. The windows will need sealing again. This is the week to do it, before the snow starts.

'He said you—'

'Bullshit.' The windows. And the door too. Fucking Sofia and her mouth. 'He didn't tell you anything.' She has this look on her face, eyes like searchlights.

The farmhouse. What could he possibly have to say about that fucking mess?

It was supposed to be empty, a routine sweep. A fuel check. Couldn't be simpler. Just the two of us going in to get any diesel they'd left.

It was quiet and it looked like no one had been there in weeks at least, so we checked around the grounds first. There was a little greenhouse at the back, tomato plants growing out through the broken glass, and a small field fenced off, the ground all chewed up by hooves. No animals in it, though. Some of the tomatoes were ripe, so I picked one and ate it while I looked around, and then grabbed another for Stefan, stuck it in my pocket. There were two old propane tanks against the house, only a tiny amount of fuel left in each. Not really worth taking. I remember looking up and noticing that all the nearby trees had their lower branches cut off, not too long ago from the look of it. I half expected to find a stack of rough fence posts or at least a woodpile if they'd cut it to burn, but there was nothing except this one branch lying on the ground near the field. It had a piece of nylon rope tied around it several times, with a tyre at the other end. A swing.

Someone had cut the swing down and then just left it there.

If there was diesel it would probably be in the old barn across the road, so I came around to the front to tell Stefan and suddenly there he was dropping to his knees, firing into the woods by the barn. It was the farmer and his brothers, his sons, whatever. Three of them. They just appeared, ran out from behind the barn and started firing at him with old shotguns. Stefan shot one of them right there, and the other two ran off into the woods. We went for it. We had to. We chased them through the trees for a mile at least, till they ran across a small clearing and turned back to try shooting at us again. We weren't that far behind and the trees were all young, just skinny, no good as cover, but getting in the way, so we threw ourselves on the ground and took them out from there, one then the other. The oldest fell last. We just lay there for a while afterwards, catching our breath, and when I rolled over I had tomato juice all down one thigh, just a load of seeds and pulp in my pocket.

We went back to the farmhouse after to look for some water and food, somewhere to just sit down and gather ourselves. Didn't realise the others were there until we were right inside. Two women in the cupboard, one with a knife and crazy eyes, a fighter, and then the other one just looking at the floor, holding a meat fork in front of her face. I didn't think, really. The crazy one stepped out of the cupboard and I didn't have time to think.

That night I found a strand of the mad woman's dark hair tangled round a button on my jacket. It freaked me out a little, like it had been cut from the head of a doll, part of a witches' spell or something. I threw it on the fire and said a prayer to Saint Dimitrije.

Sofia looks at me now like she expects some big confessional breakdown. What is it that she thinks she knows? He didn't tell her. He just wouldn't. I turn away from her and I walk over to where Mila and the kids are feeding crumbs to the ducks.

★

The others have gone to their rooms. Alan was the first to leave, slinking away after the argument, followed by Joseph. Mirko went to his after banging a few pots around on the kitchen bench.

Anna and I sit with the solar lamps facing the wall, drawing the insects away. Her head is an outline with eyes that glow just enough that I can see she is still awake. Not talking.

'Did you ever kill anyone?' Alan asked me a few weeks ago as we made dinner. Nobody spoke then, and into the sudden quiet I'd mumbled something, a non-answer.

'Don't ask me that.'

Anna's face had washed clean of any expression, eyes on the ground. Like now.

'Anna.' She's not here, not moving. 'How well do you climb trees?' She looks up at me slowly. The shadow bodies of hundreds of bugs are projected onto the wall behind her, fighting and fucking and eating and dying like an Old Testament warning.

'I used to be great at climbing trees.'

'Yeah?'

She lights up a little more in the darkness. The bugs take a second of rest, and then resume the carnage in silhouette. 'I was brilliant at it,' she says. 'Pines especially. There was one I climbed so high I could see halfway across town. One more step up and the top of the trunk would have started to bend.' She's smiling a little now. 'So what about you? You climb trees?'

'Me? Of course! You think cause I'm big I can't climb?' The whiskey's giving me ideas. Not the whiskey, the heat. Not the heat, but the heaviness. The argument. The reminders. The bullet holes in the body of the supply truck, in the body of the man who drove it. This place is giving me ideas.

I peel one finger from the side of my glass and point; the big tree crouches beside us. An escape from the ground.

Anna is standing. She puts one foot on the base of the tree, waits for me. I put down my glass. We spot a route up through the leaves and a perching spot big enough for two of us.

'Up, up!' I shout, not caring that my voice is cutting through a rare moment of quiet. She is laughing loud drunken laughs as she climbs. The tree nods its leaves – yes, yes, yes – egging us on, and I let a smile break across my face and bury itself in my cheeks.

I'm five feet off the ground, with Anna grinning down at me from above, climbing higher. Mirko appears – '…can't afford broken legs out here, get down before…' – and the applause from the leaves drowns him out. In the dim light of the lamps we can see right over the wall and through the tangle of our neighbour's razor wire. Right out into the darkness, to the dead donkey in the wadi, beyond. Every leaf bends itself back, breathes in, and chants: three, two, one – score!

I raise my right hand and fire an invisible shot into the night.

Tuti Island

Tijani fiddles with the clip of his pen as he speaks. He's normally quite calm, but today it is bad news, and so he fiddles. He explains about the problem with the unit casings, the malfunction, how it has been traced back to a manufacturing issue that has since been addressed, and as he talks, I read over my actions list and cross off this meeting. Someone from Procurement will need to schedule a follow up inspection on the supplier's end sometime soon. Maybe Tijani should go with them, just to make sure. The account manager gave him all kinds of assurances when we spoke yesterday, but we need to be certain that this was the last exploding bullet. I think about suggesting it, but decide not to. Tijani and I will sort it out later. No need to discuss every last detail here.

I lean forward and put my elbows on the table, looking down at my notes, and try to stretch as subtly as I can. Something clicks in my lower spine, a slight twinge in one hip. Tijani stands with his back to the window and, from where I am here, pressed right up against the table, I can see Tuti Island behind him, the tree line at the point where the boats come in. From street level it just looks like a stripe of green in the middle of the river, but when we fly in from above, the island is shaped like a stomach, half a kissra at the centre of the three cities. One of the ferries makes its way across the water now, bobbing like a child's toy, carrying tourists, probably. It's only a one minute journey, barely any distance at all, but that gap makes the island seem like another place entirely. Rural life right in the middle of Khartoum, like a living museum. I suppose it will all change once the bridge is completed.

Tijani finishes and Colonel Duha asks about the supplier, about whether it's been resolved. There are assurances and apologies, rather too many in my opinion – no one was killed after all, only one very minor injury, though it was the Colonel's nephew, the only reason we're even talking about it – and after a great deal of verbal contortionism and an embarrassing interjection from Rahim, the President's new secretary, we move on. At the last meeting we discussed developments in the western issue at great length and agreed to provide support on the Kurni mission, so we don't linger today. It's a matter of numbers and travel times, all of which have been arranged. The transfer of air support was made two days ago. Everything is in place, ready for my order. It's all agreed.

'We'll give it a few days, make sure our units are all back to base, and then I'll fly to Geneina for the press conference. I can stay for a week or two, if that seems appropriate. We'll take the temperature and act accordingly. So...'

There's a pause, and I smile at Rahim, guide his attention to the clock with my eyes.

'If that's everything...' I say. It takes him a second to respond, but eventually he nods and waves us out.

'Why is he even in on this? If he'd read the briefing paper he wouldn't have had to ask half of those questions.' Tijani takes the stairs with me while the rest of them continue the meeting.

'Don't worry about him. He thinks that if he talks as much as possible, he'll sound like he knows what he's doing,' I say. 'No one takes him seriously, and the thing with the bullet was just a chance happening, everyone understands that. Everyone who matters. Trust me. He might have family connections on his side, but not much else. Even the Chief knows that.'

'OK, thanks.' Tijani takes the files from me and we stop in front of the second floor door. 'Do you need anything else before you make the call?' he asks. 'If not, I've got an appointment with some pastries and at least three glasses of coffee.' He looks at his watch. 'It's long past fatur.'

'You go ahead, I'm fine. This won't take long.' He turns towards the door. 'We'll set up the inspection when I get back. I want to know that it's done properly. Enjoy your meal,' I say, and I continue down the stairs.

I've been doing this for two months now, taking the stairs, and if no one else is around when I get to the bottom, I brace my feet one at a time on the third stair up and lean in to stretch my hamstring. I think it's making a difference. I'm wary of becoming weak and corpulent now that I'm spending more time behind a desk, and each little exertion helps, I'm sure.

Today, two junior assistants from the communications office are standing in the stairwell talking about last night's news slot, Jan Pronk denouncing the war in his awkward English, so I don't stop to stretch. They pause their conversation as I pass through to the lobby. No one's really sure who knows what half of the time, or who's allowed to know, who isn't. The clever ones keep their mouths shut. Of course, Prince Rahim started his new job by dropping little pieces of information here and there, just enough to let everyone know that he was part of the inner circle. Stupid man. He should have stayed in sales.

Amal smiles at me from the reception desk as I pass through the lobby. I suck my stomach in a little and wave. I'm hungry. Maybe Tijani will save me a pastry. I scan my badge at the security doors, sign the log, and then do the same at the gates. One phone call on an outside line, shouldn't take long. If it weren't for the urgency of this call, Tijani and I could have driven over to Sahl's Grill, taken our time over a hot meal. Tomorrow, perhaps. I suppose a one-day diet won't do me any harm.

I cross the road and head towards Nile Street. It's busy today, full of scooters and Japanese pickup trucks, and the fumes hang low. The occasional armoured vehicle passes by, bulletproof body and dark tints on the side windows, but almost everyone is out in the heat today, collars open.

I cross Nile Street and find a spot in the shade beneath one of the old pines. I should call home first, tell my wife about dinner. I pull out my mobile phone and open up the contacts list. Her number is there at the top with AAA typed before it like a mechanic's sign. She must think I'm an idiot. It does make it easier though, not having to search through.

'Hi Darling, I'm just calling to ask you to get extra lamb for tonight. I want to invite Tijani for dinner if that's OK with you. He's had a bad day, a mess up at the office.'

I don't mention the trip out west to Geneina, not on her voicemail. She won't be happy. She finds Darfur stifling and backwards, and I can't really argue with that. It'll be easier to tell her in person, maybe when Tijani's there to back me up.

I hang up and drop it into my pocket. A group of students stand in a circle beneath the neighbouring tree, talking politics, all emphatic hand gestures and posturing, too close to the payphone I was going to use. I walk further along until I reach the next one that takes coins. We haven't used this one for well over a month, so it'll be fine for today. It's a quiet spot with just a couple of empty parked cars. Across the water, one of the ferries bobs alongside a jetty. Two geese are down here in front of one of the cars, beating their wings at one another and lunging, fighting over a chicken bone or something. I can't quite see what. I scuff the ground and they both jump.

The earpiece on the phone is greasy, so I wipe it down with a spare tissue and then fish through my pocket for the piece of paper. Drop the coins in, type the number for the

Western base. It rings once.

'Hello?'

I answer with the first half of the code, and he finishes it and then passes me over to the CO.

'Are you in position?'

'Yes Sir.'

'Are our friends ready?'

'Yes Sir.'

I check my watch to make sure, wait for a moment till we're on a nice even number, and then give the go order.

'Clear air support for take off and report back to me when it's done.'

I hang up, sweep the change dispenser out of habit, then walk down to the river's edge. Across the water on the far bank, the ferry revs its engine and toots its horn. A small flock of those geese take to the sky and fly upriver as if heading for the airport, and then they all lean hard to the left, turning as one, and fly back over the island in a perfect V.

Jebel Moya

Spots of water soak into my shirt as I lean over the bank of sinks and peel back the corner of the eye patch. There's a cricket ball lodged in my head, swollen from the flight, and now the edge of the patch is stuck to my cheek with a ridge of dried pus. By the time I've washed the whole thing down, applied the eye drops and changed the dressing, six other women have come and gone from the bathroom in Arrivals. I head to Baggage Reclaim and wait at the end of the Khartoum to Heathrow carousel.

At the exit gate, a throng of families stand behind the barrier, craning their necks for sight of their loved ones. Excited travellers abandon their luggage carts to run into open arms, and I pick my way through like I'm tethered to a cart.

There's Sarah, standing at the back with her arms folded. At least she came. She takes my case, out of habit, most likely, and she doesn't speak until the automatic doors open and we're hit with a blast of air.

'Are you gonna tell me why you couldn't take a taxi, or phone your mum?' she says, and she meets my eye, the good one, for the first time. 'You look like shit,' she says, and I don't reply.

I wait until we're in the car and far from the airport, the streets of London speeding past in a rain-streaked haze.

'Did you get the footage I sent?' I slide my hand into my bag as I speak, rest it on top of the camera case.

'Yep.'

She must have watched it. No matter how angry she still is, she had to at least be curious. I wait for more – questions, concern, anything – but she doesn't speak. I just need to say it.

'Sarah, I need your help.' She sighs at this, so I lay it all out before she thinks this is some desperate attempt at reconciliation. I need her to listen. 'No one else knows I have this footage. No one else has seen it.' Silence. She's listening. 'I need you to represent me.'

*

The first time I meet Dez is when I land in Sennar. He's standing outside the gate holding a piece of paper with my name on it, but I would have recognised him without it. He looks like his photo, only broader. Just as stern. I push up my sunglasses and smile when he sees me.

'Hi, I'm Jude,' I say, and when we shake hands he holds it for a second longer than is comfortable.

Although the drive from Sennar to Jebel Moya is only about twenty miles, Dez's silence stretches it. I chatter about the flight for a bit, and the small tin peacock hanging from the rear view mirror taps its tail against the windscreen with each little bump in the road. It looks like it's made from a drinks can, one of those little trinkets in the charity shops at home – 'Fairtrade and handcrafted, from Africa'. It dances a jig as Fairouz croons through the side speakers.

'I love this track,' I say. 'It always makes me think of the start of a long journey, like a soundtrack, or something.' He doesn't answer, but turns it up a little, either in appreciation, or to drown me out. I'm not sure which. I abandon the small talk and just watch the landscape pass. Shorn fields stretch out from the roadside, brown stubble to the sky's bright edge. The Blue Nile retreats behind us and soon enough, there it is: a faint smudge on the horizon that grows into a broad and flat-topped mountain. The peacock twirls and shimmies, and

126

beyond it the road dissolves in ripples of hot air. We soon reach the foot of the mountain, where we pull onto a track in the sand, a faint line that stretches around and north to the village, and when we reach the first houses, we turn up onto the mountain, the vehicle climbing alongside a seasonal stream bed that laces down onto the plain. By the time we reach the first plateau and the valley within, the waterway has narrowed. We are surrounded on three sides by mountain, the fields below lying smooth as a vast winter quilt. The world glows in evening sun.

I'm relieved to see Christine as we pull up at the site camp. She takes my hand briefly and pushes her fringe to one side. She's smaller than I remember. The last time I saw her was at the memorial service; she stood at the back and left early, didn't say much to Mum.

She shows me around the site, her top billowing out behind her as she moves. Beside the main work tent there's a small kitchen space with some insulated pots sitting on a table, bottles of water underneath. To the side are the tents, one for each of us. Home for the next few months.

'This is Liam,' Christine says. 'He'll be leading the thermoluminescence dating once we're back in the lab. He's spot dating while we're here.'

Liam is crouched down and rifling through a bag and he looks up as we approach. In that second of movement my heart stops and it's Sarah, he's Sarah – the angular face, the nose and that scruffy brown hair falling down, skin too smooth for a beard. My stomach tightens for a brief moment, and then it's gone. He stands up and offers a handshake. Face on, they're nothing alike. He looks young, younger than he probably is unless he's one of those freakishly smart kids who got their first degree at fifteen.

'I'm Jude. Hi.' His face lights up with a genuine smile when I speak.

'So, you're the artist,' he says, and I'm sure then that he's nothing at all like her.

Liam takes me over to see the old dig site while Christine makes a call on the satphone. He tells me about Christine and Dez and how he got the permit to come out here after it was refused the first time but I'm only half-listening, the rest of me focussed on the pits ahead of us, bare though they are. I've imagined this moment again and again, pictured what it would feel like to walk over here, to look down and see –

'...with the crew who are working the Merowe Dam salvage up at the fourth cataract, and the locals have asked them to pull out in support. The whole team is split. Some think they should stay, some think they should leave. One of the guys was in my graduating class.'

'Oh, right,' I say, and he seems happy with that. He continues on about this other dig hundreds of miles north, gesturing with his hands, and I soak up my surroundings. It'll be dark soon, one of those abrupt equatorial sunsets. I'll have to come back tomorrow for a proper look, but I'm grateful for these few minutes. I feel closer to Dad already. I touch the ring that hangs from my necklace and am jerked from my reverie when Liam says his name.

'He's your father, right?'

I stumble for a second, hold the ring. 'Yeah. He is.' I brace for the comment, the look that says I'm here on my last name, nepotism and nothing else, but before he can say anything more we hear a noise, a deep pulse. We both turn and watch as a helicopter heads straight for us, a dark spot that grows bigger, louder, and when it sweeps over the mountaintop we both dip our heads and hold our ears, eyes shut until the dust around us settles. When I open my eyes again Liam is squinting up into the last light.

'Weird to see a military chopper all the way out here,' he says. 'Heading for Darfur, I suppose.' We stand there listening until the sound of its blades is swallowed completely by the quiet of nightfall.

Back at camp, we eat barbecued chicken for dinner

while Christine briefs us. The topsoil's been removed and the grid set up, so tomorrow the work begins. The dig is running on a tight schedule. Most of the work will be post-excavation, which is why I'm here – on-site illustration and photography. That, along with the samples, will be crucial once the analysis gets underway back in the UK.

Christine heads straight back to the office after the briefing, and the three of us sit in silence for a moment before Liam speaks. 'Let me guess,' he says, turning to me. 'You're here because of Henry Wellcome – the aerial photography.'

I nod. 'I wrote my thesis on it. The man was a pioneer,' I say. Dez snorts, doesn't look up from his plate of food. I look back to Liam and go on. 'Well, he was the first to do it. He laid down the standard.'

'Is that why you specialised in illustration? I mean, I thought about it too, at one point,' Liam says.

'Yeah, well, that's part of it. My...' I stop myself from mentioning Dad. 'I've always been interested in the images, the representation of what has survived. The record of the record, I suppose.' Liam is smiling.

'So you will have watched all those films in the archive then, seen the pictures of his camp,' says Dez. 'Striding around like an old time missionary, Daddy knows best. Hard discipline and rules and all the tents laid out in military lines.'

'Yeah. He was a man of his time. Liked his peacock feathers, too,' I say, and Dez laughs.

'Yes he did.' He leans back and holds out his fork as he speaks. 'OK, so tell me something, Illustrator – why do you think he put so much effort into collecting, but not nearly as much into storage and analysis. Like the original site here: he brought almost all of the findings back to London and then essentially dumped them in a basement. He was dead for years before any serious cataloguing began, so what was it, for him? The thrill of discovery? Just wanting to be the first to find the treasure?' He points his fork at me like a conducting baton. 'What's your theory?'

They both watch me. 'I – I think he was looking for the origin site. Our ultimate home, I guess, as a species.' I clear my throat and neither of them speaks, so I go on. 'I think he came at it from a place of passion, and because he saw the potential of this place, of what the findings could mean, he had to collect as much as possible. Maybe he never felt like he had enough to start drawing conclusions, like there was always one more piece that was needed.'

'A constant state of preparation,' Liam says. There's that warm smile again.

'Yeah, exactly.'

'OK,' says Dez. 'So, next question – if this place was so important to the people who buried their dead here, why did they stop?' I open my mouth to answer but he goes on: 'What happened? Up north in Meroë they were building pyramids, irrigation, all the hallmarks of a powerful and unified state, whereas here in the nomadic lands, all these different people from far and wide buried their dead alongside each other for hundreds of years, all mixed together on one lone mountaintop.'

'As far as we know,' says Liam.

'Just here.' Dez leans in towards us. 'So tell me, Illustrator, if *this* place was so important to the people who moved through here, why did they stop so suddenly?'

I open my mouth and then close it. Five different sentences on my tongue and none will come out. His eyes are on me. Liam glances at Dez and then me, clears his throat. 'I think it was the Meroitic expansion...' he says.

'Wrong.' Dez claps his hands together and laughs. 'And this from our dating specialist!'

'No, I don't mean that Meroë pushed them out, of course not, the timing's not right, but as a consequence the trade route might have shifted, maybe the rise of Christianity...'

Dez isn't listening. He leans towards me with that fork bouncing the emphasis on his words. 'You need to be careful,' he says. 'You get too caught up in the peripherals – the aerial photography, rich Victorians, whatever fancy camera you've got in that bag – and you're going to miss the bigger picture.'

I don't answer. He wipes his mouth and stands over me, and I just stare at the loose thread on my knee. 'Trinity College, right?' I look up, nod. He holds my eye for a second before walking to the kitchen table, dumping his plate in the washbowl as he leaves.

In my tent, I set my lantern in the middle and unpack my case: line up the bottles of cream and hand sanitiser, stand my toothbrush and paste in a tin cup from the kitchen. I pull my scarf from the bottom and spread it out across my bed so it looks a little more like home in here. Sarah said it'd be good to have with me, versatile, and it's my favourite colour, a bright spring green, so she had to get it. That was when we were still talking. Not so long ago. I lie down on it and straighten out the corner. The gold threads at the edges catch the light.

I'm up early the next day, so before breakfast I walk across to the original excavation. The old pits are weathered and indistinct, worn down over the last century, but still visible. I can see where they would have marked it all out for the dig. Two thousand graves and Sir Henry's House of Boulders. I walk between them, slowly, letting the thrill skip up my spine. I'm actually here. My feet on the same earth, eyes on the same ground. I stop when I reach the centre and just stand there for a while, see if I can feel a pull, something like the nomads must have felt: the ancestors' final resting place, on the edge of empires. One of the papers I read called it a site of collective memory: the fulcrum of the nomads, a place that rooted them to each other, and to their past through remembering. I wonder how many remembered it. For how long? Wellcome's old pits lie empty, all that might speak long since removed.

Back at the office tent I unpack my camera and laptop, get out the sketchbooks, and my copies of the matrix sheets. Christine has the main site plan blown up and pinned to a board beside her desk. It leans towards her, its empty squares as featureless as the Gezira plain. She lifts her head above the layers of paper spread over the three work tables and waves me over as she finishes her phone call.

'Come with me.' She's straight in as soon as she sets the phone down. She marches ahead, her ice blonde hair shivering with each step, and brings me to the site edge where Dez and Liam are setting up.

'As you should already know if you've done your homework, analysis of the original findings focused on the grave goods and male remains: racial categorisation, cranial comparison, but none of it was conclusive. The most accurate thing we can say right now is that these remains represent a diverse population.' She leans on one hip and looks down at the grid before going on. 'So, we are here to gather comparative samples, and keep our minds open. No assumptions. I want summary reports each night – Dez will collect those for me – and we'll confirm work plans and deal with any arising issues at the morning meetings. 8am, in here, unless I say otherwise. I know that we're a small team, but I don't want anything slipping through because of lack of structure. You understand?' We all nod. 'We are still digging in phase as planned, sticking to sequence. Liam: I want samples of each context, one at a time, bagged, numbered, labelled and in my office before you proceed to the next. Jude, I want each feature and context photographed. Clearly, thoroughly. Illustrations too. You update the matrix, and at the end of each day it all goes on the site plan. Any problems, any uncertainty, you check with Dez, and he checks with me. The National Corporation of Antiquities and Museums will be visiting in a month to check on our progress and talk about our plans for the next season. We've got a lot to do before then. Any questions?' She scans us all with a firm eye. 'OK, I'll be in my office.'

I shoot each section of the grid as it is, seemingly bare like the site plan, and then Dez hands me a trowel. 'Time to get those hands dirty,' he says, and he turns his back.

We work on the first pit until the sun shrinks our shadows and the midday heat forces us inside. Christine drives to Sennar for a Ministry meeting and Dez sits in the shade of the kitchen space, sipping juice and reading over his notes. Liam and I set up in the office tent; he bags and stores the first of the samples while I upload the initial shots from my camera. He hums while he works.

'What's the song?' I ask.

'The Unst Boat Song.' He's got his back to me, and he just keeps working at the table, humming the repetitive tune.

'Yeah, I recognise it,' I say. He looks up.

'What, from Ancient Shetland FM?' He looks over his shoulder and laughs. 'Sorry. I just mean it sounds like a lot of other Scottish folk songs. It's probably one of those you're thinking of.'

'No, I'm sure I heard it when I was there last winter. Three people sang it acapella at one of the sessions in Lerwick.'

'Oh yeah?' He turns around then, and sits on the edge of the table. 'Do you know much about Shetland music?'

'Not really. More about the pitfalls of hitching up the main island in three feet of snow,' I say. 'Beautiful place. So harsh.' It was dark when we got in and her huge ginger cat met us at the door. The smell of peat smoke, just that one room in the house warm as an oven.

Liam watches me for a moment and then sings the first few lines of the song. 'Old Norse,' he says. 'It's a fisherman's song about a storm.'

'"Bring us safely home from the sea," that kind of thing?' I say.

'"Stronger wind comes from the wester / Curse the weather, curse the weather / Stronger wind comes from the wester / Curses from all us sailors." Something like that. There's only one line in the whole song that's in modern dialect, so most of it's a rough translation,' he says, and as he launches into an explanation of the Norse influence in Shetland music, I take a long slow breath and remember the smell, the taste in the air of that burning peat.

'Are you sure you're not Dinka? Half-Dinka?'

Amin is one of the labourers who dug out the topsoil before I arrived, and now he's on site as the odd-job man, running errands and stocking food for the cook. We've been digging for four days now, and Amin chats as I take a water break. He wants to know if this is my first time in Sudan, if I speak Arabic, where my family are from.

'My dad's from Barbados,' I say. He doesn't look convinced. 'My mum's Scottish.'

'Maybe there's a link. South Sudan – I can see it in your face. And you're tall like them too. Paler, but... ask your dad if his family came from Juba, or near there.'

'He died,' I say, and Amin immediately apologises and says something in Arabic, looks down. 'It's OK, it was a while ago,' I say, even though it wasn't, not really, but he's just nodding now. I'm about to go back to the pit when he lifts his head.

'My father died too. He's buried at the foot of the mountain. Near the village, not up here, not with the –' he waves his hand as he searches for the word – 'these old ones.' He looks out across the site. 'Will their bones go to London too?' he says, and I tell the truth.

'I'm not sure. The universities have partnered with NCAM, so the findings will probably be split – some in Khartoum, some in the UK.'

'So they won't stay here with us then, not even in Sennar,' he says, and it's not a question. Before I can respond, Liam shouts me over to the pit.

'Jude – camera.' Amin and I both go. Liam carefully dusts the soil from what looks to be the first find: three teeth in a cluster. We all lean in and beam at them for a moment. As Dez goes to tell Christine, I crouch down and shoot them as they are, smiling up from the ground. If this grave is like those on the old site, then this person was buried with reverence and care.

'I wonder if we're going to get lucky and find grave goods too,' Liam says. 'Maybe some jewellery like they found with the others.'

He draws his brush around the teeth, circling them with dust. They weren't buried with much, these people. Nomads never are. When you carry your world around with you, I suppose you choose wisely.

Amin leans in beside me, talking under his breath – mashallah, alhamdulillah, a string of praise, the kind of welcome that accompanies new babies.

'Beautiful, right?' Liam says, as I stand back for a wide shot.

'When our children lose their teeth they have to throw them up high and ask the moon to replace them with strong gazelle's teeth. Or maybe they ask the sun. I can't remember. One of them. My wife will know.' Amin leans back on his heels and stares down into the grave. 'All these different tribes lying side by side in a *perfect* burial site for hundreds of years, and then one day, or one year maybe, something changes, and –' he flicks his hand up, 'no more.'

I'm about to ask him what else he knows about the site when Dez appears beside me, his mouth set in a grimace. He grabs his tools, silent annoyance spreading out as he kneels down at the pit edge. The rest of us focus our attention on the teeth, and we don't speak.

That night, once the sun has dropped and the air cooled, I dig the thin rope from the bottom of my bag, put on my trainers, and skip behind my tent until my lungs open and my muscles burn. I'm just about finished my third set when

Christine rounds the corner, a cigarette clamped between her lips. She seems surprised, as if she hasn't heard me. She stares, and I feel like a pinned insect. I wind the rope around my hand, shift from foot to foot.

'You look like your father,' she says, eventually. 'I'm sure you hear that all the time.'

I don't know what to say, and while I search for the right words she pulls a small tin from her pocket, flips it open, and crushes her cigarette inside before snapping it shut. She watches me for a moment and then smiles like it's the end of an interview, like I'm about to be thanked, told 'We'll be in touch'. As she turns I blurt out, 'You worked with him, didn't you?' Stupid. Of course she did. I know this. She nods. I'm still shifting back and forth, my heart pounding from the skipping. My voice sounds a little funny, like I'm not enunciating properly, but I ask anyway. 'Were you with him when he – I mean, were you working in the same, *on* the same...' She's nodding. I don't know why I'm asking this, what I'm hoping for. She's as quiet as the ground. I clear my throat and unwind the rope.

'We were in Khartoum.' I hold my breath as she speaks, let it out slow and even as I wait for her to continue. 'You know already how slowly things move with the Ministry; well, after the survey was complete it took months to get them to sign off a provisional action plan, and even then we were nowhere near finalising it.' She stops and I think that's all I'm getting. Do I ask for more? At last she speaks again. 'I never liked the city but he loved... he did. Would have stayed in Khartoum if you weren't back in the UK, I think. And your mother, of course.' She stops for a moment and looks down, flicks the hair from her face.

'He'd be proud to know that you were here,' she says.

'My mum isn't, that's for sure,' I say. 'I tried explaining that Darfur and the war are nowhere near here but to her it's all the same: "the place that killed your father." I mean, he could have been hit by a car in London.'

Christine looks up at this. Again I feel pinned. I glance away and she's still studying my face when I look back. 'He would be proud,' she repeats. 'You're here finishing what he couldn't.'

It doesn't occur to me until hours later that I don't exactly know what she means. In the dark of my tent I turn it inside and out, fitting Christine's story with what I know – the secondment to the University of Khartoum and his work with NCAM, the papers on the Meroë pyramids. I know that he was Visiting Professor there, and that he died in Khartoum, road accident, 55. But what he had to do with this place, this mountain, I have no idea. Just that one photo of him in front of the House of Boulders, 'Jebel Moya Investigation' written on the back in his looping script.

Weeks go by like this. We dig, dust, photograph, sketch. No removals till each phase is as near complete as we can get it. We report to Christine, who is either pacing through a phone call, or flipping papers in her office. Liam and I tiptoe around the rolling thundercloud that is Dez, and when we talk about it, we do so secretly, at low volume.

'I think he's still pissed that she got the top job,' Liam tells me one night. He pulls the charred skin off a marshmallow and eats it, holds the shiny innards over the fire. Christine and Dez are in Sennar for the evening, a meeting or something, so tonight we're speaking freely while we eat the last of the snacks.

'His first language is Arabic, he's a specialist in the Nile basin and Meroitic culture, *and* he's got ten years on her. Did you read his article on borderlands and nomadic burial? The guy's a rock star. I've wanted to work with him for years.' Liam's marshmallow catches fire, flares, and then slides off the skewer into the coals. He swears, and reaches for another.

'Yeah, he's got the temperament to match,' I say. 'I heard him arguing with her the other day, making a big thing about how he doesn't give a shit about the management details because he's not the one being paid for it. Of course she's a massive control freak. They don't really help each other, do they?' I pull the toasted marshmallow off my skewer and we both watch the coals while I chew. 'Did I tell you my dad worked with her when she first started out? They called her "The Terrier". I think she was one of the few women in the department then. Well, those that weren't secretaries. '

'Mmm,' he mumbles through a mouthful of goo. 'You Oxbridge kids don't know you're born!' he says in an excruciating northern accent.

'Is that supposed to be Christine?' I ask, and as I laugh, my shoulders settle. We stare at the fire for a while. I turn over the coals with my skewer. 'I think she might have had an affair with my dad.'

'Really?'

'Yeah. Maybe. My mum never liked her, I know that. Christine talked to me about him right after I arrived and it was like – I don't know, like when someone's holding back, you can see the effort on their face.'

'Have you asked her?'

'God, no! I mean, what do I say? "So, were you banging my old man, or what?" I don't think I even want to know. Anyway, she'd probably tear my face off.' I look up and Liam is watching me with serious eyes. It's a relief to say it out loud.

'I'm so glad you're here,' I say, after we watch each other for a long while, and when he moves towards me, eyes on my mouth, I don't move away. I lean in. His mouth tastes like burnt sugar, his skin has a chemical tang. We kiss, and it's nice, comforting. I reach for his belly and that's when the hunger opens out like a loose hinge. My fingers curl into his skin, hook on. He kicks folders from the door of his tent as we fall in and I slide my shoes off, step on something sharp. The pain sends a bright jolt to my eye and I close it, I close them, and hold him and everything is fast and full and afterwards we lie in our sweat and we don't talk.

The short nap I intended becomes deep sleep, and I'm still on his cot the next morning when the heat of the rising sun seeps in.

'Nice ring,' he says. He's sitting on the ground at my side, staring at my shoulder. Behind my shoulder. It's slipped on the necklace and is lying on the pillow. I reach over and grab it, hold it up in front of me. My eye itches.

'It was my dad's.' I turn it over and the gold catches the sun's glow. It seems to expand. 'Moonstone. It's a little too big.' I drop it onto one of my fingers and it hangs over my knuckle, even with the chain still hanging from it. Liam smiles, turns it around to look.

'Moonstone's unlucky for men, apparently.' He looks at it for a moment longer and then leans over for a water bottle, drinks half. I finish the rest. Once I'm dressed I wait by the tent door for a moment until I'm sure that the others are nowhere nearby. I leave Liam smearing himself in factor 50 and slip out unnoticed.

I'm untying the toggle of my tent door, thinking only of getting my contacts out, when the ring slips out from under my shirt, swinging on its chain. I stand up straight to put it back and Christine is beside me, staring. She looks at the ring, and then smiles at me briefly before walking away.

After breakfast we head to the pit to set up for the day. Dez stands at a distance talking on the phone, his free hand gesturing at the ground. A moment later he strides over to the kitchen and knocks the plastic pots and cups from the table with one sweep of his arm, cursing as they bounce and scatter. He walks to where Christine stands at the office door, hands her the phone, and then spins back towards me.

'Let's go,' he shouts, as he stalks over to the truck. I had forgotten about the delivery. Liam smiles weakly, eyes full of sympathy.

'It's fine. I need to get some eye drops anyway, so it might as well be me who goes with him.' Dez starts the engine. 'You want anything?' I ask, and Liam shakes his head, whispers good luck.

We drive straight to the airport so Dez can send off the first transport box, a small one full of soil samples, and while he fills out the bill of lading I head to the Arrivals Desk. My second camera is here at last, along with the slide film. It should have arrived before I did, with the rest of the equipment, but it went missing during the transfer in Amman. I open it up and check the lens – intact. My lucky strap is in here too, tucked down at the side, along with the tripod and some extra cards for the digital.

Back in Sennar, we park at the edge of the market and Dez heads over to the bank to pick up the wages. It's crowded as usual, so I leave him waiting and slip out to the pharmacy. The smell from the sugar factory hangs thick in the air, cotton candy and burnt leaves, and my right eye waters in the heat. I've only got one contact in today, in the good eye, so the streets look like cardboard sets in a school play. A man pushes past me, gliding out towards a shakily drawn vanishing point. Women move as if on wheels, distorted and awkward like Victorian automata, and my memory slips: a room in a museum, both parents by my side.

'Edgar A. Perry's Fantastical Cabinet of Wonders'. It was our last family trip, Mum, Dad and me, and the machine was made especially for the exhibition: The Automatic Wunderkammern, telling an old story. It sat at the end of a long narrow room and it stretched from wall to wall.

A little kid catches my elbow as he runs past and I'm snapped back to Sennar, and the watering of my eye. I get two bottles of medicated drops and stand in the shade of the storefront applying them.

I've got some time before Dez will be finished in the bank, so I head into the internet cafe across the street to check my emails. I delete the spam and then open the message from Mum. It's a short note with some attached photos of the garden. Her sunflowers are now as tall as the fence, their broad heads facing down like shy teenagers. Nothing from Sarah. No surprise. I open a search page and type in her name, and then switch over to the image tab. There are hundreds of her namesakes: all ages, all ethnicities, graduation photos and glamour shots, toothy grins and wide-eyed serious stares, a tribe of Sarah Samsons. She's there too, on the second page. It's the group shot from her chambers website, all of them in suits with her in the middle, the only woman. She holds an engraved glass plaque, some kind of award. Smiling.

I type Dad's name next and he appears near the top. First is the picture from his obituary, then some others mixed in with the unfamiliar faces of other men. Most of his are posed, the kind of photos that get used for departmental websites and trade magazines: shoulders angled, face front. I skim down and at the bottom of the page is a blurry half-body shot of him with another man, an East Asian-looking guy in a suit. They're shaking hands and staring right down the camera lens, smiling. I don't recognise this one. The caption mentions Dad's name and a Wu Weisheng of Jinan Minerals, but when I click over to the host site, the browser stalls and then crashes. I refresh and try again. Nothing. The connection seems to have ground to a halt, and anyway, Dez will be done now.

It's early afternoon already, so when I meet him out on the street I offer to buy him lunch.

'Flat Chicken?' I suggest, and he nods. It's a small kitchen stall with ten or so tables arranged on the side of the road, and it's always busy. I've no idea what its real name is, but everything on the menu involves a half, quarter or whole chicken, squashed flat and cooked, with bread. I ask for no salad, and bring the plates over to the table.

We eat in silence, and by the end of the meal, Dez breathes out heavily and asks about my eye. He leans back in his chair and it feels like the tension has passed, so I tell him it's fine and then venture another topic, something neutral. 'Amin's convinced that I'm Dinka, back in the family tree somewhere. Because of my height and my eyes. Well, the good one.' A nervous laugh escapes.

Dez looks like he's not heard me, and I'm about to repeat myself when he speaks. 'I bet his kids would still call you khawaji, though.'

'He has kids?'

'Three. I met them a few times, in the village. The youngest burst into tears the first time she heard me speak her language. I tried telling her that it's my language too, but there's no point in explaining something like that to a two year old.'

'Maybe she cried because you look scary to her,' I say, and immediately wish I hadn't. I stare at my plate and brace myself as he leans across the table.

'My wife wants a divorce,' he says. Behind him, two men laugh. 'Her lawyer called this morning. She couldn't wait until I got back, apparently. She's at her sister's, and I'm here, so...'

'Oh. I'm sorry,' I say, and he shrugs, glares at his napkin for a few seconds.

'You got anyone?' he asks, and I shake my head, without thought. Before I can open my mouth to elaborate, we hear Dez's name shouted from the street. Amin. He approaches with a broad smile, another man following behind him.

'Jude, Dez!' Amin holds his arms wide, and we stand. 'This is my brother-in-law, Sheikh Raheem Gabir. I'm so pleased to introduce you.'

We exchange formal greetings with the sheikh and then Dez invites them to sit with us.

'I'm so glad we could meet like this.' Amin smiles at each of us, and places his hands on the table. 'There's something we wish to discuss with you. It's, uh –,' his voice shifts. 'It's urgent.'

'What is it, Amin?' Dez asks, and at this, the sheikh cuts in and speaks at length in Arabic. He's talking too fast for me to pick out more than a few phrases – something about the village, the mountain, going to the mountain – *dhahaba*, going, to go, I think. Maybe they need a ride back? I don't know. My language skills are awful. Dez answers him initially in English – yes; no, I haven't met him – but as the sheikh's speech becomes more emphatic Dez slips into Arabic too, the two of them leaning towards each other. Dez's face changes, hardens again, but his voice stays soft. He sits up straight against the plastic chair.

'Jude,' Amin says, 'I apologise for our rudeness. I'm sure Dez can explain it all properly. We have to go.' The sheikh agrees with him, dips his head a little towards me, and then the two of them stand abruptly and leave.

Dez waves them off, and then stands. 'We're leaving. Now,' he says, and he tucks his chair neatly under the table and then turns in the direction of the truck.

He drives fast, doesn't speak, and back at the camp the truck shakes when he slams the driver's side door. He's striding to the office.

'Christine!'

Liam stands up at the side of the pit in response and I step out into the late afternoon heat as Dez throws the office door open. His voice is amplified by the rock face at the side of the camp and I'm only a few steps closer when Christine appears at the door and gestures us over.

Dez is at the back of the tent, his feet planted wide like he's ready to spring. Liam and I both sit when Christine motions to the chairs. Dez doesn't move.

'I have to hear it from Amin!' he shouts. I glance over at Liam. The side of his face flickers where he holds his jaw tight. 'Really?' Christine opens her mouth to speak but Dez cuts her off, talking fast. 'His brother-in-law told us all about it. They haven't seen an environmental report, they haven't seen a risk assessment, almost no consultation, nothing about water security, compensation, profit share. Now they're told they can either sign a waiver or be 'resettled'. They haven't even been told where, and he asks me – this man, the sheikh, he asks me if I will hold them off. He wants me – me – to tell the company to wait. You tell me what I'm supposed to say to him. I didn't even know we were working for a goddamn mining company!' His eyes are blazing now.

'Are you finished?' Christine holds his gaze. She lets us wait in silence for a moment before going on. 'Until now the only gold mining in this area has been small scale.'

Gold. *Dhahab*. That was what I heard.

'About five years ago, the locals found a significant deposit on the east side. What looked like a potentially huge resource. The Ministry of Minerals came in, confirmed the site, and opened it up for tender. Jinan Minerals won the bid, and if I hadn't campaigned with NCAM to have it delayed for salvage excavation, these burial sites we're working now would have been destroyed.' Jinan. The muscle beneath my sore eye flutters.

She looks around at each of us, and continues when nobody speaks. 'There's nothing unusual about this process. This is standard government procedure for a development project. I was called in to oversee the completion of the salvage, and we are here to do just that. NCAM bought us time. Now we just have to recover these last remnants so that the legacy of the site remains intact.'

'As far as we know –'

Dez cuts her off. 'As far as we know these are the last remnants, and if – *if* they are, we need more than one season to finish what we've started. We're still working on the first two pits, for fuck's sake. This is not a goddamn sandbox.'

Christine juts out her chin at this and looks him directly in the eye. Liam and I remain silent in the garden chairs.

'You knew this wasn't an academic project.' Her voice is flint edged. 'You knew when I gave you the timescale, when you saw who was funding this. Cooper Evans is an investment firm for christ's sake, so don't play the righteous innocent with me. They've funded numerous other digs and they've got a solid record when it comes to supporting cultural and scientific heritage projects. You'd know that if you'd taken the time to read any of the papers I sent you. I've kept nothing from you. I've been open right from the start, so you tell me where you think I've gone wrong. Or maybe you'd rather go back to your department and lecturing undergrads for the next fifteen years.' She stares him down, and then takes a slow breath. 'Look. Jinan don't own us, OK? They do have interest in the site, but our work here is not at their bidding. I'm negotiating the next season with NCAM and Cooper Evans, and until we get that ironed out, we continue here as planned. As for the requests of Amin and the sheikh' – she looks at each of us in turn – 'you are not here to debate government policy.' Dez grimaces at this. 'If we hadn't – if *I* hadn't pushed with NCAM for this work to happen, the mine would have opened with the rest of those remains still in the ground, and who knows how much research material lost to the diggers. I'm being pragmatic, and I expect each of you to do the same.' She sweeps the room once more with her gaze. 'I suggest you get on with it.'

With that, she walks to her desk and re-engages with the stack of papers. The air is as still as the bottom of a lake and I wait for Dez to move. He throws open the door and the sunlight tears in, straight for my bad eye. A long needle of pain spikes through, and before I get up to leave, I cup one hand over it, bathe it for a moment in darkness.

When Liam sneaks into my tent that night I want to talk to him about Christine, about the mine and the village, but it doesn't happen. Afterwards, he falls asleep on my arm and starts snoring and I sort through it again and again: Jinan Minerals, the man beside Dad, shaking his hand for the camera. Wu Weisheng. When was that taken? It all starts to spin, a carousel of half-formed thoughts, until Liam shifts and frees my arm. He looks so young, especially asleep. I don't allow myself to think about what this is, me and him. I had considered telling him about Sarah and how much I thought they looked alike, but it's faded already, that brief resemblance, and anyway, I don't know how well he'd take it. Nobody likes to hear about the past like that, certainly not in comparison. She made it clear long before I left that we were done, so here we are, halfway up a mountain, the feeling slowly returning to my arm. Nothing more to be said.

'Hello? Hello?' Christine holds the phone out, looks at the screen and then sets it down on her desk. Five days have passed since we were told we are clearing the ground for a gold mine. Our pace has increased, with all of us trying to ignore the inevitable errors. The periodic discovery of new fragments is no longer inspiring celebration. No ceremony for the dead. We've started removing them from the ground, sealing them in pH neutral bags, numbering, recording and storing them in the transport boxes in the office. I'm sketching fast each day, backing it all up with the camera, and marking each item on the matrix.

I'm in the office uploading images to the server when Christine appears at the doorway. 'Come with me,' she says, and, unquestioning, I follow. She gathers us in the shade of the kitchen. Liam picks at the skin of his knuckle.

'They've moved the inspection up to tomorrow –' Dez lets out an unsmiling laugh, '– and would like us to meet with them this afternoon in the village.' She waits for a beat before continuing. 'Representatives of Jinan Minerals will be with them, and they'll be joining the NCAM inspector for the review tomorrow as well.' She pauses again, waits for dissent. No one speaks. 'Good. I told them we'll be there in an hour.'

In the back of the vehicle my eyes flicker in and out of focus, flattening everything before returning to familiar contours and shadows. The lens cap on my camera squeaks as it jostles against my trousers and I fiddle with the switch on the door, wind the window down by an inch and then up again. The peacock bounces. I think of that cabinet at the museum, a polished junk drawer come to life, Automatic Wunderkammern, and the button on the wall as we walked in. 'Push Me'. Irresistible.

I pressed the button and we stood in front of the cabinet as the curtain inside drew back. It was divided into seven sections like wings in a palace, each draped in opulent decoration, every detail colour matched – the blue room, the white room, the green room.

The whole extravagant performance would begin with the chiming of a tall grandfather clock at the far right, and as it rang out, the palace would come slowly to life. Levers pushed wheels which turned cranks, and from the floor, a host of metal people rose. A tin party. Something like a harpsichord played as the partygoers spun in bouffant dresses and shiny armour, all of them wearing animal heads. A raven danced with a fox and two in stag's heads bowed to one another. A peacock fanned its tail. At the centre of it all stood what must have been the king; he wore a fur-trimmed cape and on his head was a bright crown.

Every thirty seconds or so the clock would chime again, marking out another hour in the world of the cabinet, and the whole thing would jerk to a stop, moving again only once the count was done. Each time, the music sped up and the dancers twirled ever more urgently, moving with a desperate kind of jollity like they were holding back the dawn.

When at last the midnight chime began, a solitary figure emerged from a secret panel at the back of the cabinet. It moved out into the group, much taller than the rest, skeletal, its face pulled tight, streaks of red sweeping down from eye sockets as dark as pits. It held its arms aloft and began stalking through each of the rooms as the revellers shrank in fear.

147

The king alone stood up to the blood-eyed man, chasing him through each chamber with a dagger held high before him. They ran from the blue room to purple to green, on to orange, white and then the violet room, until at last the two of them stood before the chiming grandfather clock in the coal-dark seventh chamber. The king held up the dagger and shook with a furious rage, the harpsichord wailing a song of doom, and at that, the skeletal man turned, lifting his scarlet head high. He threw up his hands, knocking the king to the ground as though he were no more threatening than a dried autumn leaf. The guests ran forward then, a surge of clanking metal and cogs, and the blood-eyed man flew apart, piece by terrible piece, his red face last, pulled away by transparent threads. As he disintegrated, the party guests shuddered and screeched, animal heads rolling back on broken necks, mechanical eyelids fluttering. They collapsed as one at the feet of the grandfather clock, and by the end, the whole scene was a twisted mess of tin carnage. They all lay still, and a crimson light washed blood over the whole company.

The vehicle lurches over a rock in the road and my head bangs gently against the side window. On the backseat, Liam keeps turning his hand, rotating his wrist until it clicks. My lens cover creaks. I hold my breath and count as I let it out, and below the rear view mirror, the tin can peacock spins.

Dez pulls over at the side of the road. Before us are a crowd of people, and facing them, a group of bright, new Land Cruisers, each door marked with three grey triangles nested together like a mountain range. The mining reps are here, two Chinese guys, with a team of Sudanese military men and their trucks. The reps are neat and photo-ready in their business suits, and they hang back near their vehicles while the soldiers stand ahead, guns down. One of the suits talks on a satphone, the silver case flashing as he turns. He finishes the call, slides the phone into a hip holster, and glances over at us. I want him to be the man in the picture,

Wu Weisheng, to fit the pattern, slot in, but of course it's not him. I don't recognise him.

Rocks the size of footballs block the road, and behind them stand men from the village, some linking arms, some stepping out to shout past the body guards. Amin is there at the front with Sheikh Gabir, talking with two of the NCAM staff.

Dez and Christine step up to the security truck and I remove the lens cap from my camera, letting it hang around my neck. Without thinking, I hit record, squinting down at it with my one good eye. Beside me, Liam clicks his wrist – one, two – and that's when the slip happens. The sheikh pushes past the NCAM men and strides forward, and as if he's broken the skin on a spring pond, moved from water to the thin dry air, his people follow, rushing into the space he's left empty. The shouting propels them. There are legs and then bodies and then voices, a churn of cogs and pulleys, minor chord from a moaning engine, the organ in the back, and the mining men are stumbling to the vehicle, their guards closing around them, arms up and with them the rifles and when it comes, the sound is so loud that I close my good eye too, involuntarily, so loud for that instant and then the ringing like tinnitus, like an earplug pushed too far, and screaming, the screams, the people running, Liam grabbing me and pushing me down, the roar of an engine as it speeds its cargo away from the line of rocks.

My camera was still recording when we got up minutes later, but I must have been leaning right over the mic because when I watch it back that night in my tent, all I can hear is the sound of ragged breathing and Liam's voice like a robot, saying: 'OK, OK, OK.'

Amin's funeral was held at the foot of the mountain, in the village. We didn't go. Christine thought it'd confuse things, possibly upset people and I think she's right. I can't imagine we'd be welcome. Our camp is quiet, his absence tangible. We don't talk, we don't work. Liam washes his socks in a bucket. Dez sits motionless, holding a cold cup of coffee.

Christine disappears round the back of the office tent, just a plume of white smoke ascending, and when I go back there to check on her, she isn't on the phone, negotiating her way through this, she's just standing there, eyes on the sky. She offers the pack, so I take a cigarette to be polite. One drag with the lighter to start it, and then I just hold it there, watch the paper burn down ring by ring. The silence presses in.

'Have you been following much of the Darfur thing?' she says, eventually.

Darfur. The world continues away from this mountain. 'Not really,' I say. 'I mean, yeah, a little bit online, but so much of it is... I don't know. 'Arabs versus Black Africans'? That's not even... I mean, what *is* that? That language, it's so...'

'Yep. But it makes for a nice simple story, doesn't it? "Age-old tribal conflict" – the usual tired line. I'm sure they'd come to the same conclusion about the bodies here if there was any less evidence to the contrary.' She blows a long stream of smoke at the sky. 'Did you know that there were women in this ground too? High status with grave goods, low status, all of them together. They didn't get much attention in the first few rounds of analysis, but that was the '50s, so... I was hoping – am hoping to find more of them.'

She's not looking at me, but has her eye fixed on the dig site, actually just above the dig site, as if someone were standing there.

'All living and dying together, here, in the gap between empires.' She holds her arm out, points her cigarette at the pits. 'That's what happens at the borders. A gathering of people. All kinds of possibilities. It gets reduced in the retelling of course, turned inside out like a sock until it fits whatever we want, but here it is, right now, solid evidence of something special, something –.' Her voice falters and she takes a long drag on her cig. 'Ask Dez. He'll tell you.'

The ash falls from my cigarette as I wait for her to go on. She watches over the graveyard, and I'm about to speak when the phone on her hip rings.

She walks across to a rise in the rock and spends over an hour there, the phone pressed against one ear and the red tip of her cigarette flickering signals as the evening draws in. She comes back to where Liam has lit the fire as the last light leaches away to the west.

'Sheikh Gabir has asked me to suspend our work in support,' she says, 'and I've agreed.' She runs her hand through her hair. 'Neither the Ministry officials nor NCAM can confirm what unit those soldiers were with. They're saying they were private security contractors, hired by Jinan. They looked like standard government issue fatigues, but there were no markings that I remember, no flashes on any of them, so there's no way of knowing for sure. I am going to push NCAM for an inquiry into the shooting, and a full impact assessment of the site.' She looks round at us, her usual steel-eyed gaze replaced with something heavier. 'You each have your own decision to make on this, but this is the point at which I will not stand by.'

'Of course, we down tools,' says Dez. Liam and I mumble agreement. The light in the fire flares blue as I toss the last drops from my cup and wait till it settles back to orange, to red, and finally to a dull, deep glow in a pile of ash.

Before I sleep I catch Christine outside her tent. By now I'm too drunk to censor myself and it comes out, the question, an attempt at the question. My tongue is heavy and my head's confused, so the words are a jumble. 'I know he was here, with them. With Jinan, you and him. He was shaking his hand, I saw it online. I've got a photo at home, too. He was here.' I burp and cover my mouth. She doesn't speak, and I decide to slur my way onwards. She knows something. She does. 'What was he, was it Jinan? I need to know. Did he do something wrong? Why was he even here? This wasn't his area, it wasn't. It's yours. It's you. You brought him here, you were working for them and he died and, and, he was –.' My mind lurches from the centre of my argument. I can't keep still. I grab for the ring around my neck and as I hold it out she reaches for me, places her hand over mine.

'We do not work for Jinan. We never did. We answer to Cooper Evans, and more than that, to the scientific community. We were trying –' she says, and then she looks up, her eyes wide and clear. Words stick in my throat, and I spit them out like little bones, try to make her listen. She's talking too and I can't stop, need to get it out, and by the time I say it we're both shouting, me with anger, her just to be heard. I squeeze the ring as hard as I can and when the ground starts to spin I count backwards, try to reverse it. It's her fault. It has to be.

I sleep in the next day. I'm heavy on my right side as I wake, face pressed hard against the pillow. There's a tug of skin as I lift my head. The eye is glued shut. I find hot water in the kitchen kettle and hold a wet washcloth over my face. The hangover feels entirely concentrated in that one socket – dehydration and infection and the slow drum of throbbing flesh, like it has its own heartbeat.

I ease the softened pus off in stages, and then find a round gauze pad and some medical tape in the first aid kit. Double eye drops. A makeshift patch. Painkillers to dull the swelling. Liam brings food, and water. Makes coffee. He sits with me as I chew one mouthful of bread. He bounces his knee, clearing his throat again and again.

'It'll be OK,' I say, and I don't believe it. I remember shouting at Christine late last night, but not getting much back. My tongue feels like cardboard. My chest aches.

'Yeah, it's not that,' he says. He glances over at the pits. The knee starts bouncing again. Christine and Dez join us and for a while we sit together in silence. I can't look at her. It is Liam who speaks first.

'I'm worried about the remains,' he says. 'I mean, we're here now. We can get them out, make sure they're properly preserved. If we do nothing –'

Christine cuts him off: 'I'm worried too. But things have changed. A man is dead.' I flinch at this, Amin's name gone already. 'We no longer have the luxury of remaining neutral.' The phone rings, and she walks with it to the office. She stops at the door, her hand jutting out, pointing accusations at the rock face. I shut my eye, press my fingers along my cheekbone, and when I open it, Christine has returned.

She stands with us for a moment, shifting her weight from side to side, her jaw set. She stares at the ash from last night's fire. 'They're pulling us out,' she says, and the throb of my eye beats out the silent seconds that follow. Dez opens his mouth to speak and she continues: 'Cooper Evans are nervous and they don't want the bad PR, so they've suspended our funding as of today. They're in negotiations with Jinan and the Sudanese government, but for now we're out. We're to leave the site as it is, leave the office, all of the finds, and just pack up our personal stuff. They want us in Sennar tonight, for a morning flight.'

Dez starts to argue – 'Who's decision was this? What the fuck do they think –' and Christine stops him.

'We'll debrief it back in London, and will take it further there, but for now, we leave.' She looks round at each of us. 'This isn't finished. That much I know,' she says. 'Now go and pack.'

My tent is a mess, but there's hardly anything here, so it doesn't take long. I leave the cot as it is, the tent too; I'm sure we'll be back soon. I pack it all in, the scarf on the top, and then get my cameras and laptop from the office. Christine and Dez load up their gear into the back of the vehicle and I look around for Liam. He's still in his tent. Dez's face twists and he takes a step, so I cut him off. 'I'll get him,' I say. We don't need another scene.

I throw back the tent flap and there he is, sitting on his cot, his clothes strewn around like a teenage bedroom.

'Liam, we need to get moving. Come on,' I say. I kneel down beside him and grab the crumpled backpack from the foot of his bed. As I stuff the piles of clothes into the bag he starts humming the Unst Boat Song. He keeps humming, and clicks his fingers in time until I hum along with him.

'We should go to Shetland when this is done. I can be the English idiot and get my picture taken by the sign for Twatt,' he says, and I smile. 'Ah, see? I almost made you laugh. What about winter? I want to see the fire festival and all the Vikings. Get drunk in the snow.'

'Don't,' I say. 'No alcohol.' He grabs my hand and laughs, leans over and kisses my forehead.

'Sorry. You poor thing. Dez has these magic effervescent tablets and if you're really nice I'm sure he'll give you a couple of them. They're like the elixir of life, perfect hangover cures. I think they're from the Netherlands.'

He starts rummaging through his wash bag. 'In fact, I might even have some here. Let me check.' I turn and reach for a pile of folders as he chats. 'We did a trade. He's a big cigar man, did you know that?'

'Nope.'

Some papers have slipped out. I pick them up to push them back inside the folder, and there on the floor lies a small silver key ring with no key on it, just the fob. Three metal triangles inlaid with grey enamel.

'I got given a box of them when I signed but I've only smoked half of one. Too strong for me. I guess the gifts are a big cultural thing with the Chinese.'

I pick up the key ring and press my thumb against one corner of the fob. The dent stays there for a second, a perfect impression until my skin stretches back into place.

'I'll be able to make sure the site gets properly cleared, finish the salvage. There's so much more here,' he says.

The triangles look just like a mountain range. Exactly the same.

'What?'

'There's so much more here,' he says again, and the blood in my eye is banging now, a debt collector's thump, persistent and loud and he's talking, saying things about scientific resources and future legacy and Jinan Minerals and it's then, when I hear their name, the picture, the man in the suit squeezing my father's hand, grinning, and now Liam is reaching for me with one arm, his eyes huge and brown like a children's cartoon, his mouth moving and it happens, it just happens.

'You're not working for them. You're not!' I shout as I leap. It's easy to pin him with my knees, one hand on his chest and one on his head and the sound in the tent is me roaring. A metallic stream runs down my throat. My face is wet.

Red hits his nose, red on his cheek, and it's trickling down, flowing across and pooling, drawing a line to his mouth as blind rage pours from my erupting eye. I scream louder – at Liam, at the blood – and now Dez is behind me, grabbing me under the arms and when he lifts me off, the pressure pulls air into my lungs in a gasp. It comes out like a cry.

'He's, he's not –' I try to explain, but the bottom falls out and my words are gone.

*

The suite is spotless. Gleaming floor tiles stretch from wall to wall and an overstuffed leather couch sits below the window. Not how I imagined my first day in Khartoum. I suppose this is the Cooper Evans minimum standard. The NCAM liaison said that I was to help myself, so after picking through the well-stocked fridge, I pour out some water and wonder what to do while I wait. I've got a few days at least before I can fly out to Sennar and the site, just one meeting with the NCAM projects department tomorrow, so until the travel permit comes through, I've got nothing but time. I should go for a walk, check out the Nile confluence.

As I swallow the last gulp of water, I blink, and my contact lens buckles and leaps from my eye. I peer down and there it is, clinging to the side of the empty glass. I fish it out and put the glass down. There's nothing stuck to the lens, no hair or anything, so I just slide it back in and blink it into position.

I reach down for the empty glass, and through its bottom the coaster is distorted, as if the edges have been pulled up on each corner. A silver print on dark grey, the symbol shows through: three nested triangles, like a mountain range. Underneath, Arabic script. A short, elegant scribble. Unintelligible, but for two letters in English: JM. Like Jebel Moya.

I put the glass in the sink, wind my scarf around my shoulders, and, thinking only of a land halfway to the sky, I step out into the punishing heat of Khartoum.

Winter Song

WHILE I WAIT I HUM the chorus: 'and we will go with the winter sun, my dear, we will go with the winter sun'. The children run past the door of the community tent, shrill laughter in the afternoon haze, and I watch them play as I repeat the chorus twice more. I find it hard to remember the verse these days, and have to keep humming the chorus again and again until eventually I feel it coming.

One of the boys outside kicks a half-deflated football as hard as he can. It reluctantly takes to the sky and then lands with a dull thump in front of a small girl in a red dress. She's probably no more than two, chubby toddler legs spread wide, and she carefully bends down and wraps her body around the ball as the others run over to pile on, shrieking as they tumble together in the sand.

I get to the end of the chorus again, third time through, and the first line of the verse begins to form in my throat.

'We'll be with you very soon,' the translator says. He's talking with the journalist. They talk, and I wait. I agreed to the interview as long as it was here, near our shelter. I've been out walking for most of the day so I prefer to stay in the camp. I've already signed the form granting him permission to take my photo and my story, and since he's finished the photographs he packs his cameras away and fiddles with batteries on the voice recorder. He already talked to the others, before we went out. I'm the last one.

On the road, the football game has disintegrated into some kind of crawling version of chase, with the bigger children allowing the little ones to get away, pretending to grab at their toes while the young ones squeal with delight as they make their escape. Their knees leave tracks in the sand. I start humming the chorus again. Twice through, then to the verse. It was Auntie Kaia's big hit, a love song about a long winter night. They don't play it on the radio any more, not since she had to leave, but the cassettes still sell in the market. Everyone knows the tune.

The journalist is still busy with the translator, so I close my eyes for a moment and imagine them singing it, Auntie Kaia and my mother. I can picture them together at the wedding, my mother singing the harmony, but when I try to sneak up on the memory and listen in, it loops back onto the chorus. I can't seem to grab the first line of the verse. It's slipped somehow.

They're still talking. I tuck one leg up onto the chair so that I'm sitting on it, and then pull my tobe around so that it falls over my other foot, just my big toe poking out. He'll want to hear my story, the story of how I came here. It's for his newspaper in Europe. He hasn't asked the question yet but of course that's what he wants, what they all want. It's his job to ask. Where are you from? How did you get here?

I trace my toe along the edge of the faded mat on the floor. It's not a good design. Simple and badly executed, the yellows scuffed to grey, and it's coming apart at one edge. Someone should fix it. A fresh clot of blood blooms through the bundled fabric beneath me and I lean hard against my heel, think of the long answer to the question, the one that names my mother, my mother's mother, beyond, counting each of their names like beads on a string, a chain of singers: first Kaia and Nadeen, at all the best parties. I must have been about six when we went with them to the wedding. That was before Auntie Kaia left. After the ceremonies they opened the party, starting with something slow and emotional, and then

the livelier stuff with the band, everyone dancing. They sang
Auntie Kaia's new song for the first time. My sister Farah was
in charge of me that night, and when I dropped my crème
caramela on the ground she shouted at me. We didn't see
Auntie Kaia after that. She went to Khartoum to record the
winter song, and then everyone knew her. She played every
club in the capital. They loved her. Her song was on the radio
from here all the way to the Red Sea – she was even on TV
once, so we were told. She went on tour with the band after
that, concerts in Ethiopia, one in Egypt, and by the time the
tour finished, she couldn't come back.

The journalist is ready to talk to me now. He pulls two
chairs in to the other side of the table, one for him, one for
the translator, and under my breath I hum the chorus again,
slower this time. They said she'd be arrested if she came back,
beaten and imprisoned for indecency. All the musicians were
leaving. All those who could.

He leans in and smiles.

'Thank you Fahima,' he says in Arabic, and then he talks
through the translator after that.

How did I get here? Where am I from?

I think about the long answer. She sends letters from
Pittsburgh telling us that she's met some good people there,
that she sings at parties. She married the oud player from the
band, and now he drives a taxi. I make a wall of Pittsburgh at
home, next to the window where our childhood drawings
went, fitting the postcards together into an approximation of
a whole city, the one with all the bridges at the centre. There
is Auntie Kaia, one in our long chain of singers, and of course
my mother too. Before them was their mother's sister
Jumanah and her backcombed hair, performing with the jazz
bands in Omdurman. That was the '60s. Next was grandmother
and her two sisters, accomplished drummers, singing the old
songs. He doesn't need to hear all that. Unnecessary detail.
That's not what he's asking about.

The short answer.

I was singing the winter song when the planes came, but I don't tell him that bit. No need. I just start like this: Farah was with me. We were talking about Auntie Kaia's latest postcard, about how the sky didn't look real, so orange it must have been changed with a computer. We often have orange skies here, orange sunsets, but the one on the Pittsburgh postcard looked more like a painting. Farah was telling me this and I was singing the winter song and that's when the planes came in.

This is what he means. He means this bit.

We were on the outskirts of the village then and we saw them coming, so we ran down the road that leads to the hill and away. We were almost at the top when we heard the trucks ahead of us, so we turned and ran back, down to the dip in the hill where the path veers left. I rolled into the long grass, into what little cover there was, and pulled Farah down with me. When the bombs hit, they shook me from the inside. Rattled my teeth. The force of it pressed me down into the dip, an invisible hand trying to squash me, and sand was blasted into my nose and eyes. It filled my ears too, or maybe it was the sound that did that. I'm not sure.

The journalist nods as I speak, glancing at the translator from time to time. I think that was when I forgot the verse. It's since then that I can't get to it. I don't tell him that bit. Keep going. Just the facts.

We came here on foot, me and my sister, after the bombs and the things that came next, and since that time she hasn't talked. We just walked away from the village like the others, those who could. What else could we do? We just had to walk away the shame of our families. The boys were killed, the girls left to walk. That's how it was, mostly. We took it with us, walked it away from them.

We found the women's tent in the camp, and then the clinic. They helped us with what they could, told me not to worry, that we're fine. It's normal to bleed like this, two months is normal. As long as there's no pain and I'm not faint.

It happens sometimes. They checked. They'd just had a delivery from one of the NGOs, so the nurse gave me a bag of disposable cloths. I wrapped the paper bag in plastic and put it in our shelter under the mat. Farah doesn't need them. She hasn't bled since it happened.

One day, we were at the clinic for another check and I overheard one of the nurses. She said, 'That's the worst thing, the most dangerous.' She was talking to one of the other nurses. 'The wounds heal, the babies grow, but the shame just stays and hardens.'

I didn't say anything, just took the pills and the pads and the appointment slip.

I've thought a lot about what she said. About shame. I think she's wrong. It doesn't harden; it's like sand. It moves, grain by grain, never stays exactly in one place. Burns in the day, stone cold at night.

I think about telling him this, the journalist, but he just wants the facts, only what happened, and anyway now he's fiddling with the voice recorder, the translator leaning in, and they've asked me to wait again, while they fix it. Wait, just wait.

I pulled Farah into the long grass, or maybe she pulled me. I don't remember now. I think we pulled each other. After the bombs and the sand in our ears, I was lying on my side watching the sky with one eye for a while. I didn't move, just lay there, until the two of them came and lifted me up by the arms, and that's when it happened. So easy, like clicking my fingers. Without a thought I just leaned back six inches, maybe twelve, and followed behind my body. Effortless. I followed behind, singing the winter song in my head, the chorus again and again, and let my body go on ahead. Farah was there in the grass as they pulled me to the truck, and when my tobe unravelled in the wind I saw it crack like a flag, saw the dark panel of sweat soaking through the back of my shirt.

In Zero Gravity

IT WAS STILL A planet when they first met. Their first real date, if it was a date, took place on the day she heard that it was to be reclassified. They both drank coffee. She smoked, he didn't. This was long before the official announcement, only the rumblings of a few prominent astronomers, but she was angry, using the red tip of her cigarette to underline all of her arguments about gravitational dominance and Trojan asteroids and he moved the handle on his cup back and forth from one side of the saucer to the other, smiling.

They'd been sitting and talking for hours. He didn't have any particular opinion on whether Pluto should or shouldn't be a planet. It's still the same body in the same place, following the same orbit – that was his take on it. He'd never heard of its moons, but liked the sound of the nearest, Charon, and that the two of them faced each other always, sharing gravity. He said he'd name a dog after it if he ever got one, and that it was time to eat.

They walked to Ban Jelačić and sat on the steps, shovelling huge pieces of sloppy pizza into their mouths, the sunlight weakening, the night opening up, and he told her about his photographs, his favourite song and the place he'd most like to be at the moment of his death: spring evening, soft grass, looking at the sky. With a dog beside him.

Charon, she said.

Yeah. A small fleck of cheese was stuck to the stubble of his chin. His eyes were greenish brown.

Right now it's early. The light is just returning to the sky, and the tram is full. The carriage is packed with the morning shift, soon to cross over with the night workers who gather outside the kiosks, unravelling. The morning shift people look tired, mostly, cocooned in the smells of the recently woken. Too-strong deodorant hangs in the air and stale mouths leak their sighs out into the new day. One or two are alert, while the majority lean into windows and let their vision bend as the tram reaches speed and the streets outside become a blur.

The man in the green jumper is pretending to sleep, she can tell. No one will bother him if he feigns unconsciousness, and so for an extra flourish of verisimilitude he lets his window-side arm loll out from his lap. It bounces off the low shelf at the edge of the seat and knocks a flutter of leaflets to the floor.

She reads what now rests on top of her right foot. 'Instant cash!!! Our representatives are standing by to take your call.' On the other side of the window, a wasp races the tram. Usually this journey is a haze, her attention catching on nothing in particular, but today it is all detail. They pass Maksimir Park and she watches for the point that she knows up ahead, the observatory, hidden in trees. Graffiti jumps off the walls of the stadium, most of it by the Bad Blue Boys, along with 'No Profit' and 'Fuck Nato' written in large letters in English. The tram fills up at each stop, and above the shuffling of feet and bags she hears the rumble of a deep voice at the other end of the carriage. Heads turn, eyes flick up then down again, and the man in the green sweater renews his commitment to sleep with a long sigh.

They'd been together for less than a year when they moved into the place in Dubrava, a small apartment with huge rattling windows just off the main road. Dubrava felt like its own town, like Zagreb's wayward sister, scabs on its knees and plans for something big. A place for muscled dogs and fifty yard stares, its own secret language, everything negotiable.

Not long after they'd moved in, a woman stopped her outside the balloon shop at the end of their street. She wanted a light. She had a huge pile of bright bleached hair swirled around her head like a meringue, red shoes the cherries that had slid off in the summer heat. She mumbled about the children's party she had to get to and that her feet were killing her. She spoke quickly, said something about the way people walked now, faces down and what a shame it was, no one standing close enough to see the colour of anyone else's eyes, and she took in the whole city with a wave of her hand. She had huge eyelids, this woman, and a very still gaze. One of those people who looks immortally old. She lit her cigarette, then raised her eyebrows, winked, and walked off, heels clacking against the sidewalk, a pair of balloons on strings bobbing in the air behind her.

When he accepted the job, the two of them were so excited. This was the dream: his gift at capturing fleeting moments was to be applied in service of something worthwhile. All those little bits of journalism he'd done so far, the freelance articles and photo essays for the papers, the online journals, all of those had been leading to this. The contract was with Europapress Holding in Zagreb: a field posting to Sudan, reporting for the dailies. He would be heading right into the war zone, taking interviews and photos, documenting, gathering evidence that could be used to push for change and for peace, perhaps even justice. First he'd fly to Khartoum and spend a month or so working there while the permits were processed, and then he'd move westward to Darfur. Six months in all, and he would figure out a way to write home every day if he could. Plus it was way more money than he could make staying in Croatia.

Together they read the briefing papers and searched online for reports and articles on Darfur's civil war. In the early hours of the morning he fell asleep on top of a humanitarian access map; she went to the bathroom, sat on the toilet and cried.

His letters came quickly at first, sometimes in batches. They arrived full of the detritus of the city – a ticket to some Egyptian film, a lace-thin 100 dinar note – and they were full of his amazement at Khartoum.

He moved on to West Darfur, the capital city, and she received a necklace of white and black beads from the Geneina market, followed by a short email explaining he'd be out of contact, out in the field for at least two months. He gave an emergency number, a satellite phone to call if need be. Her time passed like the drip of a tap until the next message arrived, exuberant, full of his meetings with sheikhs and the brilliant material he was gathering, hard evidence in support of the hunted. He attached low-res copies of the photos he'd taken, the happy ones – kids playing with a new football, the tail end of a wedding party as they processed through a village. She printed it all off at the cafe in town and kept it in a box with the letters. They would look through it together when he returned.

The tram jolts as it pulls up to Kvatrić. In her pocket, she turns a small ball of tinfoil over and over. There's the flower stall he likes, the expensive one. Rare stalks and blooms are arranged in towers like the future of the 1920s – Metropolis in Petals. She'd need a loan to buy one of those. They hold her eye, orange and white, electric green and pink, and blood red tips of the bird-like flowers to the side. He has been away for over a year now. The messages are shorter, full of conviction. The world needs to see this, he writes, they need to know. I have never felt more certain of my work and its necessity. He attaches photos of places that look like they are made of sand, buildings the colour of the earth, bicycles wound with silk bouquets. The worst, the ones for the reports, she does not see. He doesn't want to upset her. Instead, she gets the holiday snaps. In one, his face is in the corner of the frame, grinning into the sun, and behind him the horizon stretches out like a paper cut, perfectly straight.

Something about that bothers her, looking at his still image with all that space behind him.

A few weeks before he left he drew a map for her, starting with the Grounded Sun on Bogovićeva. The first place we had coffee, he said, and so now we'll find its children. There was a whole solar system planted across Zagreb, models of each planet, and nobody knew. An artist had installed them a few years back, like some kind of secret mission, a quiet communication with the famous bronze sun that all knew so well. The first one was easy: Mercury on Margaretska, bolted to the wall of a gallery. Then came Venus, hidden away on a pillar in Ban Jelačić, and Earth, nailed to a bank. The others were harder to find, and they spent days wandering the further reaches of their city, past the tourists on the hill, out to Kozari Bok and Novi Zagreb. He left for Sudan before they got to Pluto, so she kept the map in her wallet, ready for his return.

The noise at the end of the carriage is moving closer now: a man dressed in too many coats is holding forth. The other passengers lean away and he passes easily through the path that opens around him. His head turns as he moves, nodding benevolently at each pair of down-turned eyes. His hair brushes his shoulders in stiff clumps. He murmurs continually. At Ban Jelačić, people flood out of the tram, and he holds tight to the pole, his chin jutting up. He's in front of one of the doors, and as more people cram onto the carriage he offers a greeting to each one, tilting his head, not seeming bothered by the way they slip past him without response.

The tram moves, and as she strains her head to look for Venus, the man of many coats begins to sing. There it is, just visible above the strawberry stand. Now coming up on the left, the Sun, just down there, she knows it though she can't see it. Margaretska slips by, then on the right the ice cream shop, and next comes the Earth, hidden one street away. The man in the coats raises his voice with an operatic tremble.

Everyone looks away. Everyone but her. The end of the line is pulling her and all she can do is look forward, she can only look forward. There lies Pluto, still a planet in this solar system.

The man of many coats fixes her with a powerful stare and above the rumble of the tram and the booming silence of the embarrassed hoards, he speaks directly to her: 'The king of kings is among you,' he says. She does not look away. Right at this moment, she believes him. It is all possible. She will ride this tram to the end of the line. There she will get on a bus to Bologna Alley, as far out as she's ever been. She will walk the length of it, in zero gravity if she must, to find that underpass in the fine narrow cut of the city's edge where Pluto waits, bolted to the wall, and there with a hair from her head she will hang a tinfoil Charon at its side.

Acknowledgements

The first draft of this book was written with financial support from Arts Council England, with particular thanks due to Avril Heffernan for helping me begin.

Kate Pullinger mentored me through the difficult first drafts of many of these stories, and her guidance has been invaluable. Alongside Kate's mentoring, my editor Ra Page has worked intensively with me from day one, and for his vision and commitment, I am extremely grateful.

Michael Brass' doctoral work focuses on the archaeology of the Jebel Moya site, and as I wrote its fictional story he very kindly shared his insights and writings on Henry Wellcome's dig, and the subsequent findings. In particular, his article 'Jebel Moya (Sudan): new dates from a mortuary complex at the southern Meroitic frontier' *(Anzania, Vol. 48, Issue 4, 2013)* by Michael Brass and Jean-Luc Schwenniger.

Many thanks also to Piotr Bienkowski, Dr Bernadette Lynch, and Professor Timothy Insoll for pointing the way on 'Jebel Moya', and to Literature Across Frontiers for enabling the Croatian connection through their Tramlines project with Comma Press.

Great thanks are due to Hatim Ali, who helped me with more crucial details than I can list – his fingerprints are throughout this book – and to the writers Katja Knežević and Roman Simić Bodrožić who were my guides and touchstones for the Croatian stories. To the writers of the Northern Lines Fiction Workshop: thank you all for critique, stamina and support.

About the Author

Michelle Green is a British–Canadian writer and spoken word artist who does participatory arts work in and around Manchester. Her short stories have appeared in *Short Fiction Journal* and the interactive story app *LitNav*, among other places, and her poetry collection *Knee High Affairs* was published by Crocus Books. In 2005, she worked for a humanitarian aid agency in Darfur, and the stories in this book, although fictional, are informed by that experience.